Now that the w ... k in
the sun with th ... ve
reads from Harl ...

Favorite author ...
Bought: The Greek's Bride, the first installment
in her MEDITERRANEAN BRIDES duet. Two
billionaires are out to claim their brides—but
have they met their match? Read Sandor's story now
and Miguel's next month! Meanwhile, Miranda Lee's
The Ruthless Marriage Proposal is the sensuous
tale of a housekeeper who falls in love with her
handsome billionaire boss.

If it's a sexy sheikh you're after,
The Sultan's Virgin Bride by Sarah Morgan
has a ruthless sultan determined to have
the one woman he can't. In Kim Lawrence's
The Italian's Wedding Ultimatum an Italian's
seduction leads to passion and pregnancy!
The international theme continues with
Kept by the Spanish Billionaire by Cathy Williams,
where playboy Rafael Vives is shocked when his
mistress of the moment turns out to be much more.

In Robyn Donald's *The Blackmail Bargain*
Curt blackmails Peta, unaware that she's a penniless
virgin. And Lee Wilkinson's *Wife by Approval* is
the story of a handsome wealthy heir who needs
glamorous Valentina to secure his birthright.

Finally, there's Natalie Rivers with her debut novel,
The Kristallis Baby, where an arrogant Greek tycoon
claims his orphaned nephew—by taking virginal
Carrie's innocence and wedding her. Happy reading!

Dinner at 8

Don't be late!

He's suave and sophisticated.

He's undeniably charming.

And, above all, he treats her like a lady….

But beneath the tux, there's a primal passionate lover, who's determined to make her his!

Wined, dined and swept away by a British billionaire!

Lee Wilkinson

WIFE BY APPROVAL

HARLEQUIN®

TORONTO • NEW YORK • LONDON
AMSTERDAM • PARIS • SYDNEY • HAMBURG
STOCKHOLM • ATHENS • TOKYO • MILAN • MADRID
PRAGUE • WARSAW • BUDAPEST • AUCKLAND

ISBN-13: 978-0-373-12641-5
ISBN-10:   0-373-12641-7

WIFE BY APPROVAL

First North American Publication 2007.

This edition published by arrangement with Harlequin Books S.A.

® and TM are trademarks of the publisher. Trademarks indicated with ® are registered in the United States Patent and Trademark Office, the Canadian Trade Marks Office and in other countries.

www.eHarlequin.com

Printed in U.S.A.

All about the author...
Lee Wilkinson

LEE WILKINSON attended an all-girls school, where her teachers, often finding her daydreaming, declared that she "lived inside her own head," and that is still largely true today. Until her marriage she had a variety of jobs, ranging from PA to a departmental manager, to modeling swimsuits and underwear.

As an only child and avid reader from an early age, Lee began writing when she, her husband and their two children moved to Derbyshire. She started with short stories and magazine serials before going on to write romances for Harlequin Mills & Boon.

A lover of animals—after losing Kelly, her adored German shepherd—she has a rescue dog named Thorn, who looks like a pit bull and acts like a big softy, apart from when the postman calls. Then he has to be restrained, otherwise he goes berserk and shreds the mail.

Traveling has always been one of Lee's main pleasures. After crossing Australia and America in a motor home, and traveling round the world on two separate occasions, she still, periodically, suffers from itchy feet.

She enjoys walking and cooking, log fires and red wine, music and the theater, and still much prefers books to television—both reading and writing them.

CHAPTER ONE

SEATED at her desk in her first-floor office, Valentina Dunbar was gazing absently through the rain-spattered window which overlooked Cartel Wines's long, narrow car park and, beyond the high wall, the River Thames.

Dusk had begun to creep stealthily out of hiding and lights were coming on, gleaming on the dark water and glowing orange against the cloudy purple sky.

Most of the day staff tried to get away early on a Friday night and a steady stream of vehicles were already leaving the car park to join the London evening rush hour.

Responsible for organising the social gatherings and the informative literature that invariably accompanied Cartel Wines's latest sales push, Tina was endeavouring to put the finishing touches to the pre-Christmas campaign. But for once she wasn't giving the job her full attention.

It was Friday the thirteenth. A day that, for her at least, had lived up to its unlucky reputation.

First thing that morning she had slipped and hurt her ankle getting out of the shower. Gritting her teeth, she had been forced to stand on one leg while she had dried and dressed and taken her thick, silky hair, naturally blonde on top but with darker undertones, into a neat chignon.

By the time she'd finished, the pain had eased quite a bit

and she was able to hobble into the living-room to get her toast and coffee.

Ruth, her friend and temporary flatmate, who was breakfasting in her dressing gown, looked up to ask, 'Why are you limping?'

As Tina finished telling her, the phone rang.

'I hope this is Jules,' Ruth exclaimed eagerly, grabbing the receiver.

It was.

Her fiancé's firm had transferred him to Paris for six months and she was missing him badly.

'He's coming to London for the weekend,' she said after a minute or so, her elfin face full of excitement, her black hair standing up in spikes. 'He'll be arriving this afternoon and going back Monday morning.'

Then, apologetically, 'By the way, he's expecting to stay at the flat with me…'

The 'flat' was nothing more than a large bedsitter, which meant that Tina would have to make other arrangements for the three nights.

Her own flat was in a run-down Victorian house that the new owner had decided to have refurbished and modernized, and Ruth had offered her a put-you-up for the ten weeks or so that would elapse before she could move back in again.

'Perhaps you could ask Lexi or Jo to give you a bed for the weekend?' Ruth suggested.

'I'll think about it,' Tina said non-committally. Then, seeing Ruth's concerned expression and knowing she owed it to her friend, she added cheerfully, 'Don't worry, I'll get something fixed up. You just make sure you have a great time.'

'I will,' Ruth assured her as she went to shower and dress.

Both Lexi and Jo had resident boyfriends and, with no intention of playing gooseberry, Tina had already made up her mind to book into a hotel.

As soon as she had pushed a handful of underwear, a few changes of clothing and some necessities into a small case, she collected her shoulder bag and mac and, calling, 'Have a good weekend…see you Monday,' let herself out.

When she had descended the stairs with care, she crossed the foyer to check for mail. In Ruth's pigeon-hole was a single redirected letter addressed to her, which she thrust unopened into her bag.

Until now the autumn weather had proved to be glorious, an Indian Summer of warm golden days and balmy nights. But today it was grey and chilly, a thin curtain of drizzle being blown along by a strong blustery wind.

She turned up the collar of her mac and, her ankle still a little painful, made her way to where her car was parked in the *residents only* space that belonged to the building.

Her offside front tyre was flat.

By the time the local garage had checked the tyre, repaired the damage and re-inflated it, she was late for work.

The morning had passed in something of a whirl and it had been practically twelve o'clock before she'd realised that, owing to the earlier upheaval, she had forgotten to pack her usual sandwiches or her small flask of coffee.

But there was a delicatessen just around the corner that made up rolls and sandwiches to order. If she could get there before the rush…

As she reached in her bag for her purse she came across the forgotten letter. Glancing at it, she noticed that in red, on the left-hand side of the envelope, was stamped what appeared to be the name of some firm.

Dropping it on her desk to read when she got back, she pulled on her mac and made her way out of the rear entrance.

In a few minutes she returned, carrying a ham and salad roll and a fruit yogurt in a paper bag. She was crossing the deserted car park, her head down against the now driving rain when, glancing up, she saw a man watching her.

Tall, dark-haired and arresting, he was standing quite still beneath the roofed loading bay, his eyes fixed on her.

Since Kevin's defection, shattered and wholly disillusioned, she had steered well clear of all men. Especially handsome ones.

Though this man couldn't be called handsome in the film star sense. He was very good-looking but in a tough, wholly masculine way.

Her pulse rate quickening, she found herself wondering who he could be.

As she drew nearer, their eyes met.

Some glances were like collisions. The impact of those dark eyes stopped her in her tracks and made her heart start to throw itself against her ribs.

She was still standing rooted to the spot, staring at him as though mesmerized, when the bottom of the wet paper bag gave way, allowing her lunch to fall through.

The roll, though soggy, was fairly easy to pick up, but the plastic yogurt carton had split and its contents were oozing out.

Making use of one of the paper napkins that had been included, she managed to scoop up the mess and deposit the remains of her lunch in the nearest litter bin.

As she wiped her hands on the remaining napkin, her gaze was drawn once more to where the dark-haired stranger had been standing.

With a strange sinking feeling in the pit of her stomach, as though she had dropped too fast in an express lift, she found herself staring at the now empty space.

He had vanished.

She was certain he hadn't passed her and she had neither seen nor heard a car start, which meant he must have gone inside.

So who was he?

She knew all the admin and general office staff by sight and this man didn't belong to either. Nor, she was quite sure, was he one of the warehouse staff. Apart from an unmistakable air of assurance and authority, he had been far too well-dressed to be doing manual work.

However, to have been here at all, he must have some connection with Cartel Wines.

Perhaps he was a visitor.

But visitors always used the visitors' car park and the main entrance. They didn't come in the back way and go through the warehouse, as he must have done…

A trickle of icy-cold water ran down the back of her neck, making her shiver. Belatedly aware that she was standing like a fool getting saturated, she hurried into the building.

As she walked through the warehouse she glanced about her. But there was no sign of him amongst the men at work and she knew she couldn't mistake him.

When she reached the top of the stairs she found that her office door was a little ajar and realised that in her haste to beat the rush she couldn't have latched it properly.

While she fetched a towel from the small adjoining cloakroom to pat dry her hair and face, her thoughts winged their way back to the dark-haired stranger like homing pigeons.

In spite of the fact that she had seen him only briefly, his height and the width of his shoulders, the image of his lean, attractive face was clear in her mind. And, though she had tried her hardest to dismiss it, it had haunted her for the rest of the afternoon, displacing any thoughts of hunger.

Now, gazing through the window, her blue-violet eyes abstracted, she was still wondering about him… Who was he? Why had he been here? If he *had* been a visitor, would she see him again…?

But she must stop this fruitless speculation, she told herself sternly, and concentrate on practicalities. At almost five o'clock on a wet Friday afternoon, with darkness hovering in the wings, she still hadn't decided where to stay.

But after urging Didi, her stepsister, to accept the place at the prestigious Ramon Bonaventure School of Drama that she had been offered, and promising to pay her fees, it would have to be somewhere not too expensive.

Still, she would manage somehow. It might mean stringent economies for a couple of years, but to have Didi—who had been christened Valerie, but had always been Val to her friends and acquaintances and Didi to her family—on course again it would be well worth it...

The bleep of the internal phone cut through her thoughts. Pushing aside the lists of dates and tasting notes that littered her desk, Tina picked up the receiver.

'Miss Dunbar,' Sandra Langton's somewhat nasal voice said, 'Mr De Vere would like to see you before you leave.'

'I'll be straight down.'

Wondering at the unexpected summons, she left her office, a slim figure in a smart grey suit, and, still limping slightly, descended the flight of bare stone steps that led down to a wide corridor.

On the right, the heavy double doors into the warehouse—where the wines for the domestic customers were stored before being put into stout cartons to be despatched nationwide—were closed.

To the left were the main offices. In the outer office, Sandra Langton, the boss's middle-aged PA, gave her an odd look before saying, 'If you'd like to go straight through?'

Frowning a little, Tina tapped at the door of the inner sanctum and waited for the curt, 'Come in.'

She thought, not for the first time, that if Frenchmen were noted for their charm, Maurice De Vere had to be the exception to the rule.

A short, dry man with grey hair, thin features and an irascible manner, he was due to retire at the end of the month.

He hadn't really been a bad boss, she reflected, but, a diehard who disliked modern technology, he had refused to install computers or any equipment that would have made office life easier.

Added to that, he had always believed in the stick rather than the carrot, so whoever took his place would almost certainly be an improvement.

Ensconced behind a large, imposing desk, with a motion of one claw-like hand he waved her to a chair.

She was barely seated when, looking down at a sheaf of papers, he began, 'I'm afraid I have some bad news for you, Miss Dunbar...'

He hesitated, then, looking at her over his rimless glasses, went on abruptly, 'When I decided to retire and I sold out to the Matterhorn group, they promised very few changes. On the whole they've kept their word. But this afternoon I learnt that John Marsden, the man who'll be coming in on Monday to start running Cartel Wines, has his own very definite ideas about how the sales campaigns should be staged.'

'I don't see that as a problem,' Tina said quietly. 'The suggestions I've already made can easily be changed or adapted to suit—'

The words died on her lips as De Vere began to shake his head. 'I'm afraid Marsden's insisting on bringing in his own team of organisers, which means you're redundant.'

As she stared at him in stunned silence, he added, 'I'm more sorry than I can say. Your work has always been excellent...'

Coming from a man who had never been known to compliment his staff, that was praise indeed. But what use was it when she was now out of a job?

'Bearing that in mind, I'll make sure you have very good references.'

'When…?' Her voice wobbled dangerously and she stopped speaking.

Looking uncomfortable, he said, 'As Marsden will need your office for his own team, it would be best if you left immediately. I've authorized six months' salary in lieu of notice, which will be paid directly into your bank…'

That was very generous. Her contract had only specified one month.

'A reference and any other appropriate papers will be sent to your temporary address in due course.'

Rising to his feet, he held out his hand. 'May I wish you well.'

Her voice under control now, she said, 'Thank you,' then shook the cold, papery hand and walked out of the room with her head held high.

In the outer office, Sandra Langton, who was just putting on her coat, said with obvious sympathy, 'Tough luck.'

Then, dropping her voice, 'I must admit I was surprised by how hard old Sourpuss took it… When will you be leaving?'

'Now… As soon as I've cleared my desk.'

'Well, all the best.'

'Thank you.'

Shock setting in, Tina climbed the stairs on legs that felt as wadded and useless as a rag doll's and, sinking down at her desk, gazed blindly into space.

She had been with Cartel Wines since she left college two years ago. It was a job she had loved and been good at. Even old Sourpuss—as the staff called De Vere behind his back—had admitted it.

But that made no difference whatsoever. Due to circumstances, she was now unemployed.

A kind of futile panic gripped her. Six months' salary was a buffer, but when the alterations to the house had been completed and she moved back into her flat, her rent would be considerably higher. That, added to Didi's expenses, meant losing her job couldn't have come at a worse time.

Over the past year, life had been a series of downs with scarcely any ups. Now, with this final blow, she seemed to have hit rock-bottom.

Well, if that *was* the case, the only way was up.

Allowing herself no more time for regrets, she rose, squared her shoulders and started to tidy her desk top.

Only when it was clear, did she suddenly recall the letter she had been going to read. Seeing the handsome dark-haired stranger had put it right out of her mind.

But where was the letter?

A quick search through the papers she was taking failed to bring it to light.

Oh, well, it must be there somewhere. She would look more thoroughly later.

Finding an almost empty box in the cupboard, she transferred the few remaining items in it to one of the shelves, then, taking her personal belongings from the desk drawers, stacked them in the box.

The plants she had brought to brighten the somewhat spartan office, she would leave.

She pulled on her coat, put the strap of her bag over her shoulder, tucked the box under one arm and, switching off the light, closed and locked the door behind her for the last time. There was nothing of value in the office, so she left the key in the lock.

Just the night security lights were burning, which meant that the rest of the staff had already gone and she was probably the only person still left in this part of the building.

The main entrance doors at the front would have been locked and bolted some time ago. But her car was in the rear car park, so it was just as quick to go through the warehouse.

As, without looking back, she began to descend the stairs to the dimly lit passage, a movement she *heard* rather than *saw* made her realise that she had been wrong. There *was* someone else still here.

At the bottom of the stairs she turned right and in the gloom saw that the double doors at the end of the passageway were swinging slightly.

Whoever was still here was obviously only a little way in front of her and heading for the car park, as she was.

When she went through the doors, however, the long warehouse appeared to be deserted.

More than a little puzzled, she frowned and, her footsteps echoing in the vast space, began to walk past the various bays, with their rows of pallets stacked with crates and boxes of château bottled imported wine.

Last autumn and winter, on the nights she had worked late, she had walked through the warehouse without a qualm. But tonight, for no good reason, she felt on edge, uneasy.

The night security lighting was high up in the roof of the building and left areas of deep shadow that suddenly seemed sinister, providing as they did an opportunity for someone to lie in wait…

She was doing her utmost to ignore the far from comfortable thought, when some sixth sense insisted that she wasn't alone, that someone was watching her from the shadows.

The fine hairs on the back of her neck rose and her skin goose-fleshed. Instinctively, she paused and glanced behind her.

Not a soul was in sight.

Gritting her teeth, she was about to walk on when in the silence she heard a faint noise like the brush of a furtive footfall.

The echoing vastness of the warehouse made it impossible to tell where the whisper of sound had come from.

She was standing rooted to the spot when she realised that it would be George Tomlinson, the night security man.

Feeling foolish, she took a deep breath and called out, 'George, is that you?'

Only the echo of her own voice answered.

She tried again, louder.

Still no answer, apart from the mocking echoes.

It occurred to her that he was probably doing his early evening rounds of the offices, checking that all the lights were out and the doors locked.

But if it *wasn't* George she'd heard, who was it?

Perhaps someone had slipped in through the small door the employees used and had been heading for the wages office when they had heard her coming and decided to hide?

Reason soon put paid to that theory. It was Friday night and, as any would-be thief would undoubtedly know, Friday was pay day and the safe would be empty.

After a moment she recalled that there were a couple of cats who lived on the premises.

But cats moved silently and they didn't go through heavy doors and leave them swinging.

A shiver ran down her spine at the memory.

Don't be a fool, she chided herself sharply; it was time she used her common sense rather than letting her imagination run away with her.

Instead of someone going out ahead of her, it must have been George, coming the opposite way to check the offices, who had left the doors swinging.

It was a perfectly logical explanation.

Yet, illogically, she didn't believe it.

Well, whether she believed it or not, it was high time she made a move.

If George had already locked up and completed all his checks—he wouldn't have worried about a light in her office; he was used to her working late—he could well be ensconced in his little cabin on the far side of the annex, having his tea.

Which meant that he might not emerge until it was time to

do his rounds again and she couldn't stand here much longer. Her ankle hurt and the box under her arm was getting heavy.

Glancing round her, she could see no sign of life or movement. Still the feeling of being watched persisted, as though the watcher was patiently waiting to see which way she would jump.

She pushed the thought away and, summoning all her will-power, decided that as she had already walked more than half the length of the warehouse it made sense to go on, rather than turn back.

Fighting down a panicky impulse to run, she forced herself to walk steadily towards the huge sliding doors at the end of the hangar-like building.

Her legs felt curiously stiff and alien, her breathing was rapid and shallow and every muscle in her body had grown tense. Try as she might, she was unable to stop herself from glancing repeatedly over her shoulder.

When she reached the small staff door to the left of the big main doors and found it securely closed, she breathed a sigh of relief. It boasted a Yale lock so, unless someone had a key, it could only be opened from the inside.

So much for some thief slipping in and hiding! With an over-active imagination like that, she should be writing stories...

Her tension relaxing, she let herself out into the dark, wet night and closed the door carefully behind her. Everywhere appeared to be deserted, though a dozen or so cars remained and, outside despatch, a couple of Cartel's vans were waiting to be loaded.

The pre-harvest sales push had been phenomenally success-ful and extra orders for hotels and restaurants were being dealt with by a special evening shift working over in the annex.

Beyond the range of the annex's lights, however, the car park, poorly lit apart from the entrance, had areas that looked pitch-black.

Having come in almost an hour late that morning, she had been forced to park in one of the old, narrow, brick-walled bays that sloped steeply down towards the river. None of the employees used the bays if they could help it because of the difficult manoeuvring that was entailed, and the fact that they were at the far end of the car park.

There wasn't a soul in sight as she began to limp to where she'd left her car, but once again she felt that uncomfortable *awareness*, that disturbing sensation of unseen eyes watching her, and a tingle of fear ran down her spine.

She felt a cowardly urge to head for the annex where there were lights and people…

But then what would she do? Admit that she was scared to walk through the car park alone? They would think she was mad.

And they wouldn't be far wrong, she thought crossly as, resolutely ignoring her fear, she carried on. Perhaps all the stress of the last year had caught up with her and was making her paranoid? If so, the sooner she got a grip the better.

Unable to see more than a few yards ahead, it took her a moment or two to locate her small navy-blue Ford. When she did, it was a relief to put her carton on the back seat alongside her case and slide behind the wheel.

There! Safe! So much for these stupid fancies.

As she started the engine and began to back out, it occurred to her that she still had no idea where she was heading.

For someone who was…*had been*…paid to organise things, she wasn't doing too well on her own account, she told herself wryly. But, for once in her life, she hadn't been thinking straight, otherwise she would have looked for somewhere in-expensive and booked before she'd left the office.

Her left ankle had stiffened up and she was finding it painful to use the clutch, so it would be as well if she could find some-where comparatively close.

As she started to turn, it occurred to her that there used to be a smallish hotel a couple of streets away. Now, what was it called…? Fairfax? Fairhaven? Fairbourn? Yes, that was it. She couldn't remember noticing it lately, which might mean that it had closed down, but—'

From behind there was a sudden dazzling blaze of headlights and a glancing rear impact sent the front of her car swerving into the wall with a grinding of metal and a tinkling of broken glass.

Momentarily paralysed by shock, she was sitting motionless when the driver's door was jerked open and a male voice demanded urgently, 'Are you all right?'

'Yes… Yes. Quite all right…' Her own voice seemed to come from a long way away.

The car had stalled when her foot slipped off the clutch but, even so, he reached inside and felt for the ignition key to turn everything off.

'Then I suggest you stay where you are for a minute while I assess the damage.' He closed the door against the rain.

Though she felt dazed, part of her mind registered that his voice was low-pitched and pleasant, a cultured voice and not one she recognised.

But that attractive voice had said, *'while I assess the damage'*… She groaned inwardly. From what little she could see, his car appeared to be a big expensive one. And, though he had hit her, she was to blame. If she had been concentrating, instead of thinking about where she was to stay, it might not have happened.

She had just managed to gather herself and was about to unfasten her safety belt and climb out, when the door opened and he was back.

'How bad is it?' she asked fearfully.

'The original impact was only a glancing blow, so there's hardly a mark on my car…'

She could only be thankful for that.

'But I'm very much afraid that the damage caused when your nearside front wing hit the wall will make your car undriveable.'

After the kind of day she'd had, it was the last straw and she gave way to a crazy impulse to laugh.

His face was in deep shadow and she couldn't see his expression but, sounding concerned and obviously wondering if she was about to become hysterical, he asked, '*Sure* you're all right?'

'Quite sure…'

A shade apologetically, she explained, 'I was just seeing the funny side. It's been an awful day and I'm afraid I'd reached the stage where I either had to laugh or cry.'

'Then you made the right decision.'

As he held the door against the wind, a scattering of rain blew in.

Suddenly realising that he was standing getting wet when, but for her, he would no doubt be on his way home to his wife, she made to clamber out, favouring her bad ankle.

He stepped back and put a steadying hand beneath her elbow.

Startled by his touch, she said jerkily, 'I'm really very sorry about all this…'

'As my car hit yours, I'm the one who should be apologizing,' he told her.

Honesty made her insist, 'No, it was my fault. My mind was on other things and when I started to back out I hadn't realised there was anyone else about.'

'Rather than stand in the rain arguing,' he said dryly, 'I suggest that, for the moment at least, you allow me to accept the blame. Later, if necessary, we can always agree on six of one and half a dozen of the other.'

Opening the door of what, at close quarters, she could see was a top-of-the-range Porsche, he added briskly, 'Now, before you get wet through, suppose you jump in and I'll take you home.'

'That's very good of you, but I…' Her words tailed off as,

in the glow of his headlights, she recognised the dark, powerful face she had thought never to see again.

When, her wits scattered, her heart starting to race, she stood rooted to the spot, he said, 'Is there a problem?'

When she didn't immediately answer, he suggested, 'Perhaps you don't trust me?'

'No… No, it's not that.'

'Then what is it?'

She blurted out the first thing that came into her head. 'I— I was just wondering if I should try and move my car.'

'Leave it where it is,' he told her decidedly. 'It shouldn't be in anyone's way and first thing tomorrow morning I'll get my garage to tow it in and do the necessary repairs.

'Now, is there anything you need out of it?'

'A small case on the back seat.'

'Jump in and I'll get it.'

He had left the engine running and in a moment she was installed in the warmth and comfort of the most luxurious car she had ever been in.

Not even Maurice De Vere had a car in that class.

She found herself wondering what a visitor—and, as she had never seen either him or his car before, the dark-haired stranger *must* be a visitor—was doing in Cartel's car park so late in the evening…

Her case deposited in the boot, he slid in beside her and reached to fasten both their seat belts. That done, he turned to her and, in the light from the dashboard, studied her face.

Embarrassed by his close scrutiny and only too aware that with wet, bedraggled hair and a shiny nose she must look an absolute fright, she felt her cheeks grow warm.

As though sensing her discomfort, he moved away a little and asked, 'Where to?'

'I—I don't know,' she stammered.

He raised a dark brow. 'Amnesia?'

Knowing he was making fun of her and vexed with herself for losing her usual calm composure and acting like a fool, she took a deep breath and said crisply, 'Certainly not.'

Pulling a mournful face, he observed, 'Oh, dear…now you're mad with me.'

For an instant she wavered between annoyance and amusement. Amusement won and she smiled.

Smiling back, he observed, 'That's better.'

His smile increased his charm a thousandfold and she found herself thinking that a lot of women would find him irresistible…

Suddenly becoming aware that he'd asked a question she hadn't caught, she pulled herself together and said, 'I'm sorry?'

'I asked *why* don't you know?'

Trying to be brief and succinct, she explained, 'Well, the house I live in is being refurbished, which means my flat is uninhabitable, and I'm staying with a friend…'

He listened, his dark eyes fixed on her face.

Thrown by the intentness of his gaze, she momentarily lost the thread.

Then, realising he was waiting, she carried on a shade distractedly, 'Her boyfriend is in London and expecting to stay with her. But her flat is really only a bedsit, so you see I have to find a hotel.'

It seemed like a heaven-sent opportunity and, his thoughts racing, he said, 'That shouldn't be a problem. There are plenty of hotels in London. You don't have any particular preference?'

'No, anywhere will do… So long as it's not too expensive,' she added hurriedly.

But, judging by his clothes and his car, he wouldn't have to consider expense, so he was hardly likely to know any of the cheaper places. And she couldn't expect him to go touring London on her behalf when he'd already been held up and inconvenienced.

Recalling her earlier thought, she said, 'I'm not sure if it's still there, but there used to be a small hotel quite close to here, on Mather Street… I think it was called the Fairbourn…'

His well-marked brows drew together over a straight nose. 'If it's the place I'm thinking of, I wouldn't say it was particularly prepossessing.'

So long as it was clean and respectable, she wasn't in a position to be over-fussy. 'As it's only for three nights, I can manage.'

Three nights suited his purpose even better, he thought jubilantly.

Things had been going smoothly, but the business trip he'd been forced to take had cost him precious time and they had managed to trace her much faster than he'd anticipated.

Hence the sudden need for drastic action.

Which had worked so far, he reminded himself. But with so much at stake, he simply couldn't afford to mess things up.

'As the Fairbourn may well have closed down,' he said smoothly, 'and it's hardly the sort of night to be touring the town in search of accommodation, I suggest you come home with me.'

CHAPTER TWO

WHEN, staggered, wondering what he had in mind, Tina simply stared at him, he repeated evenly, 'Come home with me.'

Knowing what kind of woman she was, he hadn't expected much in the way of opposition and was shaken when she said, as if she meant it, 'I couldn't possibly do that.'

'Why not? There's a perfectly good guest room standing empty.'

Though she was reassured by the mention of a guest room, there were other considerations. A mature man in his late twenties or early thirties, he might well be married. 'Thank you,' she began, 'but I—'

'It makes sense to come for tonight at least,' he broke in decidedly. 'Then tomorrow, if you want to move into a hotel, you'd have all day to find somewhere suitable.'

Rather than ask if he was married, she said, 'What on earth would your wife say?'

'As I don't have a wife, not a lot.'

He hadn't a wife. Her spirits rose with a bound.

Then common sense took over. If he hadn't a wife, he would almost certainly have a live-in lover.

'But you must have… I mean there must be…'

'A woman around?' he supplied quizzically.

'Well…yes.'

'Oh, there is.'

Though she had half expected it, her heart sank.

'Thank you,' she said carefully. 'It's very kind of you to suggest it, but—'

He sighed. 'Now I've put you off and I thought you'd feel easier, knowing there was another woman around the place.'

She shook her head. 'I really think I should go to a hotel. It'll be far less trouble for—'

'Oh, Gwen won't mind,' he said easily.

If *she* was living with him she wouldn't be too happy if he brought a woman home he didn't even know. Decidedly, she began, 'I'm quite sure your girlfriend would—'

'Oh, Gwen's not my girlfriend. She's my housekeeper. A very upright woman,' he added solemnly. 'A pillar of the church and so forth.'

Feeling as though she was on a roller coaster and with the disturbing impression that he was enjoying teasing her, Tina frowned.

'Is that a problem?' he asked, straight faced. 'Do you have anything against religious women?'

'Of course not,' she began. Then, seeing the wicked gleam in his eye, she stopped speaking and gritted her teeth.

'In that case it's all settled,' he announced calmly and let in the clutch.

He had managed it so smoothly that they had pulled out of the car park and joined the evening stream of traffic that flowed down Lansdale Road before she could gather her wits enough to assess the situation.

Though she was very attracted to him and *wanted* to be with him, the voice of caution warned that to meekly go off with a man she knew nothing about was reckless in the extreme.

Just because he was well-dressed and well-spoken and had a big expensive car, it didn't necessarily mean that he was trustworthy.

As her mother would have phrased it, he might have designs on her.

Though why should he?

She was tall and slim with good skin and neatish features, but she was nothing to write home about, certainly not the sort to drive men wild.

And a man with his looks and charisma wouldn't be short of lady friends. In fact, with so much going for him he wouldn't need to lift a finger to have eager females queuing up.

But, apart from that, there was something about him, she felt, a kind of basic integrity that was oddly reassuring. And this might well be her one and only chance to get to know him. If she insisted on being dropped off at a hotel, in all probability she would never see him again.

The thought was like a hand squeezing her heart.

It didn't seem possible for a quiet, self-contained woman like herself to feel so strongly about a man she had only just met and didn't know.

Yet she did.

Throwing caution to the wind, she asked, 'Where do you live?'

His build-up of tension relaxing, he smiled. 'I've a house in Pemberley Square, close to St James's Park.'

'Oh…' A far cry from Mather Street and the Fairbourn Hotel.

'As we'll be spending the night…' He paused. 'I was about to say *together*…but, as that might be misconstrued, I'll say *under the same roof*, I think we should introduce ourselves, don't you? My name's Richard Anders.'

'Mine's Tina Dunbar.'

'Tina?' He sounded surprised.

'Short for Valentina,' she explained reluctantly.

He gave her a sideways glance and, his voice casual, asked, 'Is Valentina a family name?'

'No.'

'Born on February the fourteenth?'

She nodded. 'That's right. Though these days Valentine is used for either sex, unfortunately my mother preferred to stick with the feminine form.'

'Unfortunately?'

'Valentina is a bit of a mouthful.'

'I like it.'

'Oh…' She felt a little warm glow.

As they headed for the West End, the wipers rhythmically swishing, the wet, almost deserted pavements reflecting back the brightly lit shop windows, he said, 'So you're with Cartel Wines… What do you do, Valentina…?'

Very conscious of him, of the handsome, clear-cut profile, the closeness of his muscular thigh to hers, the faint male scent of his cologne, she tried to drag her mind away from the man himself and focus on the question.

'Are you a buyer?'

'No. I'm responsible for public relations and sales promotions.' Then, with a sinking feeling, 'Or, rather, I *was*.'

'You're leaving?'

'I've no choice. I learnt this afternoon that Matterhorn, the group who have taken over Cartel's, have their own promotional team coming in next week, which makes me redundant.'

'So you won't be going back?' he pursued.

'No. I've cleared my desk.'

'Have you been working for Cartel Wines long?'

'Ever since I left college,' she answered without thinking.

He gave her a quick sideways smile. 'As you look about sixteen…'

Wishing fruitlessly that she looked her usual cool, composed self, she said quickly, 'I'm twenty-three,' and was aware that she had sounded indignant.

'That old!'

Now he was laughing at her openly. But it was in a nice way, a way that invited her to join in.

With a smile, she said, 'I suppose in a few more years being told I look about sixteen will seem like a compliment.'

Then, keen to remove the spotlight from herself and wondering what he'd been doing at Cartel Wines, she changed the subject by remarking, '*You're* not employed by Cartel?'

'No.'

'I didn't think so. But I wouldn't have put you down as a visitor. Or certainly not an ordinary one.'

'Is that a complaint or a compliment?'

'A comment. Ordinary visitors use the front car park and the main entrance and always leave before the staff.'

'Well, as I did none of those things, I plead guilty to being out of the ordinary…'

It occurred to her that she still didn't know why he'd been at Cartel Wines, but, before she could pursue the matter, he remarked, 'Incidentally, I caught sight of you earlier in the day…'

So he'd recognised her.

'Yes, I'd slipped out to buy some lunch.'

To give her no chance to ask the question that he wasn't yet ready to answer, he went on, 'I fear it came to a sad end. Did you manage to replace it?'

'No.'

'You must be ravenous. But we'll soon be home and Gwen's sure to have dinner waiting.'

Wondering how the housekeeper would cope when he turned up with an unexpected guest, Tina began, 'I'm afraid it—'

'Don't worry,' he broke in, 'there'll be no problem.' Then, deciding to stick with a safe topic, at least for the moment, he went on, 'As a young woman, Gwen had a family of six boys to feed, so she's always been used to cooking for what seems like an army. She still does.

'Her church runs a centre for the homeless and each evening she fills her car boot with food and takes it round there.'

He had just finished telling her about his housekeeper's charitable activities when they reached Pemberley Square and drew up outside a handsome porticoed town house.

It was still raining hard and he retrieved Tina's case before escorting her across the leaf-strewn pavement and into a chandelier-hung hall.

As he closed the door behind them, a small, thin, neatly dressed woman appeared.

'Ah, Gwen,' he said, 'we have an unexpected guest.' He introduced the two women, adding, 'Miss Dunbar was with Cartel Wines.'

The housekeeper smiled and said, 'I'm pleased to meet you, Miss Dunbar.'

Smiling back, Tina said a little anxiously, 'I hope I'm not causing you a lot of trouble, Mrs Baxter?'

'Not at all. The guest room is always kept ready. Now, if you'd like to freshen up before dinner…?'

'If there's time?'

'Plenty of time,' the housekeeper announced comfortably. 'Luckily I'd decided on a casserole, which will keep hot without spoiling.'

'In that case,' Richard said, 'I'll check my emails and when Miss Dunbar comes down we'll have a quick pre-dinner drink in the study.'

With a glance at his watch, he added, 'But, so your regulars won't have to wait too long for their supper, I suggest you leave ours on the hotplate and we'll serve ourselves…'

Mrs Baxter nodded gratefully, then said, 'Oh, there's one more thing… Miss O'Connell has been trying to get hold of you. She said your mobile has been switched off all day. She seemed extremely upset about it…'

Reading his housekeeper's tight-lipped expression correctly, Richard hazarded, 'So Helen's been giving you a hard time? Sorry about that.'

Her face softening, Mrs Baxter said, 'The young lady would like you to give her a ring.'

'I'll do that. Thanks, Gwen.'

Taking Tina's case, the housekeeper led the way up a long, curved staircase and across a balustraded landing, remarking as they went, 'Mr Anders is always kind and thoughtful. They don't come any better.'

Doing her best not to hobble, though her ankle was, if anything, worse, Tina asked, 'How long have you worked for him?'

'Just over six years and in all that time I've never known him be anything other than even-tempered and pleasant.'

'That's praise indeed.'

'And well earned. He's one of the most generous people I know.

'In the two years that it's been in existence the centre that I help to run must have saved quite a few lives, especially in the winter.

'They have him to thank. Not only did he buy a big warehouse and have it converted into comfortable living quarters, but he pays all the running expenses out of his own pocket and provides money for food and other necessities.

'He's even managed to save a few of the poor souls who come there... Oh, not by preaching to them, but by trusting them and giving them a decent job...'

Tina was about to ask what kind of business he was in when she was ushered into a large pastel-walled bedroom that overlooked the rain-lashed lamplit square, with its central garden and mature trees.

Having deposited the case on a low chest, the housekeeper closed the curtains, remarking, 'It looks like a nasty wet, chilly night, so I'd best get off and make sure that everyone's taken care of.'

Her hand was on the latch when she turned to say, 'Oh, when you come down again, the study is straight across the hall.'

The guest room was pleasant and airy, with a pale deep-pile carpet, modern furniture, a large, comfortable-looking bed and walk-in wardrobes, while the *en suite* bathroom was frankly luxurious.

Feeling grubby and dishevelled, Tina decided to take a quick shower.

While she enjoyed the flow of hot water over her bare skin she thought about Richard Anders.

Any remaining doubts about what kind of man he was had been set at rest by Mrs Baxter's unstinting praise and she could only be thankful that she had accepted his hospitality rather than turning it down.

Refreshed, she towelled herself dry, quickly found some clean underwear and swopped her suit for a fine wool button-through dress in oatmeal.

Her ankle was distinctly swollen now so, instead of changing into high-heeled sandals, she stayed with her flat shoes.

When she had put on a discreet touch of make-up and brushed and re-coiled her dark blonde hair, she made her way carefully down the stairs.

She felt eager and excited, if a touch nervous, at the prospect of spending the evening alone with Richard Anders and getting to know him better.

For perhaps the first time in her life she found herself wishing that she was clever, beautiful, exciting, alluring— whatever it took to arouse and hold his interest.

But of course she wasn't. She was just an ordinary girl, unable even to keep the interest of a man like Kevin who, though undeniably tall and handsome, hadn't been in the same class as Richard Anders for looks and presence.

But perhaps it was wealth that had given him his presence, his force of personality?

No, she was oddly convinced that it wasn't so. If he'd been a poor man he would still have had those assets and, with them, he wouldn't have remained a poor man for long.

Arriving at the study door, after a momentary hesitation, she tapped and walked in.

It was a pleasant book-lined room with a rich burgundy carpet and matching velvet curtains. An Adam fireplace and an ornate plaster ceiling with flowers and cherubs added to its beauty.

The lighting was low and intimate and a log fire blazed cheerfully in the grate. A small table and a couple of soft leather armchairs had been placed in front of the fire.

Richard, who had been standing by the hearth, advanced to meet her. He looked coolly elegant and just the sight of him made her heart lurch wildly.

He too had made time to shower and change. Instead of the business suit and tie he'd been wearing, he was dressed in smart casuals. His thick dark hair was brushed back from his high forehead and his jaw was clean-shaven.

'So there you are. Come and make yourself at home.'

A hand at her waist—just that impersonal touch made her go all of a dither—he ushered her to the nearest chair.

Trying to look cool and composed, she sank into it.

His glance taking in the touch of make-up, he smiled at her and said teasingly, 'My, now you look all of eighteen.'

That white smile, with its unstudied charm, rocked her afresh and made her feel as though her very bones were as pliable as warm candle wax.

'I'd just started to wonder if you knew which was the study,' he went on, 'or if you were wandering around, lost.'

'No, I knew. Mrs Baxter told me.' She was aware that she sounded more than a little breathless.

Indicating a drinks trolley, he queried, 'What's it to be?'

Bearing in mind that she'd had nothing to eat since breakfast, she plumped for orange juice.

While he added crushed ice to the glass and poured the freshly squeezed juice, she watched him from beneath long lashes.

In dark well-cut trousers and a black polo-neck sweater, he looked even more handsome and attractive and, in spite of all her efforts, her heart began to pick up speed.

He glanced up and, unwilling to be caught staring, she looked hastily away.

A moment or two later he was by her side. Handing her a tall, narrow, frosted glass, he said, 'Here you are.'

While she sipped, he leaned against the mantel, a whisky and soda in his hand, firelight flickering on his face, and studied her appraisingly.

He would have expected the sort of life she'd been leading to have left its mark, but at close quarters she looked clear-eyed and healthy and altogether too *untouched* to be the kind of woman he knew her to be.

He'd known from the start that she was blonde and blue-eyed, had even seen photographs of her, which had convinced him that she was attractive.

But the first time he had seen her in the flesh coming out of De Vere's office he had realised that the photographs didn't do her justice.

She was beautiful.

Now, taking in the long-lashed blue-violet eyes that slanted slightly upwards at the outer corners, the lovely silky hair the colour of corn-syrup—and natural too, he'd bet—winged brows and high cheekbones, the straight nose and the mouth that his own suddenly felt the urge to kiss, he revised his earlier opinion.

She was more than merely beautiful.

Much more.

She was bewitching, haunting, a fascinating contradiction. Despite that passionate mouth, she had an air of innocence, of vulnerability that, however false, had got under his skin the instant he saw her. And that could be dangerous.

He shrugged off the thought.

Being attracted to her was all very well so long as he kept in mind what his goal was and didn't allow that attraction to affect his judgement.

Over the past few weeks he had considered several courses of action. But, thinking it would be easier to judge when he knew her better, he had been waiting to decide exactly how to play it, which would be his best option.

In the end, however, things had moved so fast that he'd had no time for a leisurely appraisal.

Still, most of his plans were in place, even his final contingency plan. Which, because of the time element, he was now going to have to go with.

If he could bring it off.

There was no *if* about it. He *had* to bring it off.

But, having seen her at close quarters, he knew that taking her to bed would be no hardship. In fact the mere prospect made his blood quicken.

Of course, if he could get her *emotionally* involved, make her fall in love with him, it would ease his task enormously.

Experience told him that she was already attracted to him, though oddly enough she wasn't giving out the kind of overt signals he would have expected from a woman like her.

He knew from the reports he'd received that she was, to put it mildly, a child of her times and, despite her air of naivety, he found it almost impossible to believe that she had any scruples or inhibitions.

But, as time was short and he was unwilling to take any chances, it would do no harm to make certain that *if* she had, they were well and truly banished...

Tina glanced up and, thrown by the expression of almost savage intensity and purpose on his face, asked jerkily, 'Is something wrong?'

'Wrong? Of course not.'

His voice sounded quite normal and the expression that had

startled her was gone as if it had never been. Realising it must have been a trick of the firelight, she breathed a sigh of relief.

Straightening, he asked easily, 'Another drink?'

'Please.'

Taking her glass and moving over to the drinks table, he said, 'I suggest this time you try it with a secret ingredient.'

Curiously, she asked, 'What *is* the secret ingredient?'

He gave her a lopsided smile. 'I have to confess that it's nothing out of the ordinary. Merely a dash of Cointreau.'

She laughed and took a sip of the drink he handed her. As he stood looking down at her, she saw for the first time that his eyes weren't simply brown, as she'd thought, but a dark green flecked with gold. Handsome tawny eyes, with long heavy lids and thick curly lashes.

As she gazed up at him, he took the glass from her hand and set in down on the low table. Then, stooping unhurriedly and as if—rather than obeying a sudden impulse—he knew exactly what he was doing and could take all the time in the world to do it, he kissed her mouth.

She had been held closely and kissed many times. But never like that. Without holding her in any way, with only their lips touching, his kiss held everything she had ever wanted— warmth, tenderness, passion, sweetness. It both gave and took, coaxed and effortlessly mastered.

When finally he lifted his head and drew away, she felt radiant, enchanted.

Satisfaction in his voice, he remarked, 'I've been wanting to kiss you since the first moment I caught sight of you standing there in the rain.'

Though—now she had seen his house—common sense told her he was right out of her league as far as any serious relationship went, she was filled with pleasure and excitement. He'd felt the same kind of instant attraction that she'd felt and, for the moment at least, that was enough.

Though it could lead nowhere.

And it was dangerous.

Especially if Richard had seduction on his mind. And, after the way he had kissed her, she could no longer rule that out.

But she wasn't one to have affairs or indulge in casual sex, so if he *did* intend to try and seduce her, she would just have to stay cool and uninterested.

Cool and uninterested! Who was she trying to kid?

So she would have to *appear* to be cool and uninterested. In the past she had always been good at quietly freezing men off, she reminded herself. But then she had been *genuinely* uninterested or, for one reason or another, unwilling to take that particular relationship any further.

Though it was old-fashioned, almost ludicrous in this modern age, she had been brought up to believe that love and commitment went hand in hand and that sex should belong within the framework of marriage.

It hadn't made her narrow-minded or critical of other people's behaviour. It was simply a standard that had been set for her and that she had so far adhered to.

While some of her friends laughed and said she was mad and others admired her, Ruth had suggested it was because she had never been seriously tempted. 'No, I haven't forgotten Kevin,' she had said, 'but while he was tall, dark and handsome, he obviously hadn't got what it takes to turn you on.

'It's a jolly good thing you didn't marry him,' she had added seriously, 'otherwise you might have ended up just going through the motions and missing out on one of life's most wonderful experiences...'

'Penny for them...'

Richard's voice brought Tina back to the present.

Her cheeks growing warm, she stammered, 'I—I was just thinking about something my friend said.'

'You're not angry that I kissed you?'

She shook her head.

Sounding confident, he added, 'And I take it there's no current boyfriend to object?'

A little piqued by that assumption, she said, 'What if there is?'

With a kind of wry self-mockery, he told her, 'If there is I'll have to wrest you from him…'

She had the strangest feeling that he would be prepared to wrest her from the archangel Gabriel himself should it prove necessary.

'Is there?'

She shook her head.

'But you didn't like me assuming that?' he queried shrewdly.

'As it happens, my fiancé and I split up earlier in the year.'

He raised a brow, not expecting her to have had such a serious past relationship. 'How long were you engaged?'

'About three months.'

'Officially?' he queried.

'You mean did I have a ring?'

He looked casually down at her left hand. 'Did you?'

'Yes.'

'Who broke things off?' Richard queried.

'I did,' Tina answered.

'Why?'

She paused, then looked up at him. 'I caught him playing around with another woman.'

'Do you still love him?'

'No, I don't,' she said, and knew it was the truth.

'But you still feel upset about it?'

She *had* until now. Though it wasn't so much that it had happened as the *way* it had happened.

Realising he was waiting for an answer, she said, 'I did at first, but now it no longer matters.'

Suddenly wondering if her words had been too revealing and feeling uncomfortable, she began to sip her drink once more.

Nursing his whisky and soda, Richard sat down on the other side of the hearth and changed the subject with smooth aplomb. 'I understand the sunny summer and autumn they've had on the Continent has helped to produce an excellent grape harvest…'

While they talked about the good weather they'd been enjoying and the climate in general, though he barely touched his own drink, an attentive host, he refilled her glass once more.

At length he rose and, having put some fresh logs on the fire, remarked, 'We'd better get something to eat before you starve to death.'

As they walked to the door, he told her, 'The dining-room is at the other end of the hall.' Adding, as she favoured her injured ankle, 'Can you manage?'

A little flustered, she said, 'Oh, yes, thank you.'

'Sure? I can see your left ankle's swollen and I've noticed you limping from time to time.'

'I'm sure I can manage, thank you.'

The gold and ivory dining-room was elegant, the table laid with cut glass and porcelain, while a bottle of wine encased in a silver cool-jacket waited to be poured.

Dinner, though simple, proved to be most enjoyable. Richard played the part of host with panache, filling Tina's plate and helping her to some of the excellent white wine.

Somewhat to her relief, he chose impersonal topics of conversation and as they ate they discussed books, music, art and the theatre. It didn't take long to discover that their tastes matched in most things and they both much preferred reading to watching television.

'I sometimes think television is the bane of modern living,' he observed, 'especially when the set takes over the room and becomes the focus of it.'

She agreed entirely and said so.

By the time the leisurely meal came to an end and Tina

had finished her second glass of wine, starting to feel distinctly light-headed, she elected to take her coffee black and refused a liqueur.

It was getting late by the time their cups were empty but, knowing it made sense not to rush this part, he led the way back to the study.

Having stirred the glowing fire into life and settled her in front of it, he suggested, 'Let's have a small nightcap before we turn in.'

As, hazily happy just to be here with him, she was gazing into the flames, he handed her a balloon glass containing a swirl of golden cognac. Then, taking a seat opposite, he raised his own glass in a kind of toast and took a sip.

When she followed suit, he asked conversationally, 'How did you hurt your ankle?'

'I slipped when I was getting out of the shower.'

'Hardly a good start to Friday the thirteenth,' he commented dryly, 'and I gather things didn't improve very much?'

'Not a lot,' she said and, when he waited expectantly, went on to tell him about having a flat tyre and being late for work.

'Then at lunch time I discovered I'd forgotten to pack any sandwiches…'

He shook his head sympathetically. 'And, after losing your lunch, you end the day with a badly damaged car and no job.'

Though having no job still had to be a major worry, it didn't seem half so bad now she was sitting opposite Richard, sleepily watching the flickering firelight turn his face into a changing mask of highlights and shadows.

Hoping she hadn't sounded sorry for herself, she said hardily, 'But it could be worse. Mr De Vere has promised me a good reference, so it shouldn't take too long to find another position.'

'I presume you know a lot about wine?'

'Quite a lot,' she said simply. 'Otherwise I couldn't have done my job.'

Studying her reflectively, he queried, 'Any idea where tonight's wine came from?'

'France,' she answered without hesitation. 'I'd say the Loire Valley.'

'Can you put a name to it?'

Recognising that she was a bit squiffy, she said cautiously, 'Yes, I believe so.'

When he waited, one eyebrow slightly raised, she correctly named both the wine and the year.

Looking surprised, he remarked, 'Surely you weren't able to learn how to identify the area and the vintage merely from tutorials and course work?'

Sensing faint disparagement, she said, 'No, of course not.' Then, realising that she was starting to slur her words, she made an effort to enunciate more clearly. 'That has to come from the hands-on side, the bouquet and tasting…'

She stopped speaking, feeling dazed, overcome by tiredness. All she wanted to do at that moment was lie down and go to sleep.

Watching her trying to keep her eyes open, he said, 'You look more than ready for bed.'

He rose and in one lithe movement put the fireguard in place.

'I'm sorry…' she began.

'There's nothing to be sorry about. It's been a long, eventful day…'

He was right about that, she thought as she struggled to her feet.

'Need any help?' he queried.

'No, no…I'm fine,' she lied as, limping, she wove her way somewhat unsteadily to the door. Oh, why had she accepted that cognac? She should have had more sense.

Having bided his time until she reached the hall, he said firmly, 'I think I'd better carry you.'

Not at all sure that she'd heard him aright, she echoed, 'Carry me?'

'Carry you,' he repeated firmly.

Going hot all over at the thought of being held in his arms and cradled against that broad chest, she stammered, 'R-really there's no need. I can manage quite well.'

Her normally low, slightly husky voice sounded agitated and squeaky.

Ignoring the assurance, he stooped and effortlessly lifted her high in his arms.

With a little gasp, she begged, 'Please put me down.' Adding distractedly, 'What on earth will your housekeeper think if she sees us?'

Looking unperturbed, he said, 'No one will see us.'

'How can you be so sure?'

'Because Jervis, the chauffeur and handyman, lives at the rear above the garages, and Gwen, who used to be a nurse, is staying at the centre overnight. Old Tom, one of her "regulars", is just recovering from a bad bout of flu, so she's remaining on hand in case he needs her.'

'Oh,' Tina said in a small voice.

As he crossed the hall and began to climb the stairs, Richard smiled down at her and added with soft emphasis, 'So you see, we're all alone.'

CHAPTER THREE

ALL alone.

Just for a second Tina had the absurd feeling that she'd walked into a trap.

There had been something in his voice, his choice of words—satisfaction? a touch of menace?—that made her heart start to thump against her ribs and a shiver run through her.

Noticing that betraying movement, Richard glanced down at her. 'There's no need to look so scared—' now his tone was reassuringly normal '—I haven't lured you here to imprison you in the cellar or lock you in the attic…'

Suddenly feeling foolish, she denied, 'I never thought you had.'

'Though I do have plans for you.'

The rider, though added jokingly, brought a touch of alarm.

'Plans?' she said thickly. 'What kind of plans?'

He laughed. 'Don't worry; I'm sure you'll like what I have in mind.'

Realising that he was teasing her, her head spinning, she let it go.

He carried her easily and when they reached the top of the stairs there was still no sign of him being out of breath.

As well as strong, he must be very fit.

Virile was the word that sprang to mind. It was a word that immediately produced some erotic images…

Shocked by her own thoughts, she told herself hazily that this wasn't like her. It must be alcohol swamping her inhibitions. Normally she drank very little and the amount she'd had tonight, some of it on an empty stomach, had gone straight to her head. As he crossed the landing and fumbled briefly to open her bedroom door, everything began to whirl gently round her and she closed her eyes.

Crossing to the bed, he pulled back the duvet and laid her down, supporting her head while he unfastened the clip that held her heavy coil of hair in place.

As the silken mass tumbled around her shoulders, he settled her head on the pillows and, sitting down beside her, slipped off her shoes.

She lay like a beautiful doll, her eyes closed, the long lashes making dark gold fans on her cheeks, her soft lips a little parted, the lovely creamy column of her throat exposed, vulnerable.

It was obvious that the alcohol had done its work too well and she was almost out for the count.

Frowning, he realised that she couldn't be as used to drinking as he'd been led to believe. It had been his intention to get rid of any possible inhibitions, not to make her practically incapable and he felt like a heel.

However, he couldn't afford too many scruples. Everything he held dear was at stake. If he'd been certain she would be reasonable…

But he *couldn't* be certain. It would depend entirely on what kind of woman she really was, and he wouldn't know that until he knew her better.

By that time it would be too late.

So he needed to go through with it.

As he made the decision, she opened her eyes.

Smiling down at her, he started to undo the buttons of her dress.

He had reached her waist when, pushing herself up groggily and brushing his hands away, she said hoarsely, 'It's all right... I can manage.'

'Sure?'

'Quite sure.'

'But you would like me to stay.' He made it sound as if it had all been decided.

The true answer was yes.

But even in her tipsy state she knew that all he wanted was a one-night stand and, making an effort to stick with her long-held principles, she started to shake her head.

It was a mistake and, as the world began to spin once more, she closed her eyes and mumbled, 'I'd like you to go.'

'Then I'll say goodnight.' He leaned forward and kissed her.

The light pressure of his lips against hers was enough to make her sink back against the pillows.

His mouth still keeping contact, he followed her down and, when her lips parted helplessly, he deepened the kiss until her head was whirling even more and her whole being melted.

Without conscious volition, her arms went round his neck and she was holding on to him as if he were the only stable object worth anything in her world...

Her brain came to life slowly, consciousness ebbing and flowing. As she lay with closed eyes, she became aware that she was unusually warm and comfortable on the rather uncomfortable put-you-up.

And, what was even more unusual, her hair was loose around her shoulders—normally she braided it—and she was naked. Why wasn't she wearing her nightdress? Unable to think, she let the thought go and drifted off again.

It was the sound of a shower running that eventually began to penetrate her stupefied state.

Ruth must be up early this morning. Usually she was last in

the bathroom, preferring to breakfast in her dressing gown even on a weekday.

But surely this was the weekend? Hadn't it been Friday yesterday?

Friday the thirteenth and everything had gone wrong...

Like a tide carrying flotsam, the events of the day washed into her mind and for a moment or two she sorted dazedly through them until she found the one thing that mattered above all else.

She had met Richard Anders.

The recollection banished sleep and focused her attention. A moment later, memory filled in the details with a rush.

The car accident, the invitation to go home with him, the drive to Pemberley Square, his kiss in the study, dinner together, brandy in front of the fire... Then him carrying her upstairs after saying with a strange intonation in his voice, 'So you see we're all alone.'

He had taken her into her room, laid her on the bed and kissed her goodnight...

But she had a vague memory of wanting him to stay, of kissing him back and putting her arms around his neck... Her eyes flew open and she sat bolt upright.

She was briefly aware that the room was light, sunshine slanting in through a gap in the curtains, then, the sudden movement making her head spin, she groaned and, squeezing her eyes tightly shut, pressed her fingertips to her temples.

'Headache?' a male voice asked sympathetically.

She opened her eyes again to find Richard just emerging from the bathroom. His dark, attractively rumpled hair was still damp from the shower and he hadn't a stitch on.

The sight of that beautifully toned male body with its muscular chest and lean hips, its trim waist and taut belly, made her heart lurch wildly and her stomach tighten.

Oh, but he was gorgeous. A superb male animal.

As she gaped at him speechlessly, he strolled over and, bending, kissed her lightly on the lips as if he had every right.

As if they were lovers.

Which, no doubt, they were, otherwise what was he doing in her room stark naked?

Transfixed by the thought, she froze.

When, sitting still as a statue, she failed to respond to his kiss, he looked at her appraisingly, trying to sum her up.

He knew what kind of woman she was and, though he was sure that she wanted him, she wasn't acting as he would have expected. Most of the women he had known would have twined their arms around his neck and done their best to coax him back to bed.

But, instead of trying to look seductive, she looked positively embarrassed, as if she wasn't used to sleeping around.

Had she reacted like those other women, he would have accepted the invitation. Even first thing in the morning and with a hangover, she was the most beautiful woman he had ever seen.

Her neck was long and slender, her breasts small and firm, with dusky-pink velvety nipples that he felt the urge to stroke with his tongue…

Realising that his eyes were fixed appreciatively on her breasts, in a panicky reflex action she jerked up the duvet to cover her nakedness.

A gleam of amusement in his eyes, he said, 'I'll get you something for that headache.'

As he turned and walked to the door, she caught her breath at the seductive back view of his tall, well-built figure.

His skin, with its golden all-over tan, was clear and glowed with health, his shoulders were broad, his buttocks firm, his long legs strong and straight. The line of his spine was elegant. Even the back of his neck, with the damp hair trying to curl a little into his nape, was sexy.

The thought of the housekeeper catching sight of him leaving her room naked made Tina exclaim, 'But what will Mrs Baxter think if she—'

Further amused by this show of propriety, he turned and said,

'I'm not expecting her home for a while. I told her I'd rustle up some breakfast and she could take as much time as she needed. So no doubt she'll stay and feed her flock.'

Grinning, he added, 'By the time she gets back, rather than shock her, I'll be dressed and my bed will look suitably slept in.'

A second later the latch clicked and he was gone.

With a strange hollow sensation in the pit of her stomach that she identified as shame, Tina sat and stared at the closed door.

Last night she had obviously waved goodbye to her principles and enjoyed what Ruth had called 'one of life's most wonderful experiences' *and she couldn't remember a thing*.

Now, as well as feeling ashamed, she felt cheated.

If she hadn't had too much to drink…

But if she hadn't had too much to drink, she reminded herself grimly, she wouldn't have slept with him in the first place.

She knew from the way her contemporaries talked that that kind of thing wasn't uncommon, but she had never expected it to happen to *her*.

Well, now it had and it was too late. What was done couldn't be undone. She would just have to live with the shame.

She bit her lip.

If they had known and loved one another it would have been different… Or if there'd been any promise of a serious relationship…

But neither of those things applied.

It had been purely and simply a one-night stand. On his part, at least.

From a kaleidoscope of emotions, anger and dismay and regret at her own behaviour stood out.

She almost wished she could say he'd taken advantage of her but, recalling the way she had put her arms round his neck and clung to him, in all honesty she couldn't.

He must think she was easy, that this was her usual behaviour. Cringing, she wondered how she was going to face him.

And he would be back before too long.

The mere thought turned her insides into a quivering mass of jelly.

Trying to get a grip, she told herself bracingly that she was bound to feel better, more confident, when she had showered and got dressed.

Averting her gaze from the chair that held last night's discarded clothes, she stumbled out of bed. The movement made her temples pound so violently that for a moment she was forced to stand with her eyes shut, too dizzy to move.

When the world stopped spinning, she located her clip on the bedside cabinet and fastened her hair on top of her head.

Then, moving more carefully now, both for the sake of her head and her ankle which, though a great deal better, still wasn't quite right, went into the bathroom to clean her teeth and shower.

While the hot water and lavender-scented gel flowed slickly over her bare flesh, it occurred to her that, in the circumstances, she would have expected her body to look and feel different— a faint redness here and there, a little stiffness, some tenderness perhaps? '*Fulfilled, more like a real woman,*' would have been Ruth's poetic way of putting it.

But, apart from a headache and feeling slightly nauseous, which were obviously the effects of too much alcohol, there wasn't a mark on her and physically she felt just the same.

Only nothing *was* the same.

It never would be again.

As she dried herself and cleaned her teeth, trying to ignore the fact that in a single day her whole world had somehow been turned topsy-turvy, she made what plans she could.

Richard Anders had promised to get her car fixed so, hopefully, if she gave him Ruth's address, the garage would let her know when it was done.

In the meantime she would leave Pemberley Square as soon as possible and book into a hotel.

Though her heart plummeted at the thought of walking away from Richard, it was something she *had* to do. If she looked as if she was making any attempt to cling or prolong things he would only secretly despise her…

She had just returned to the bedroom to find some fresh clothes when a tap at the door sent her scurrying back into bed.

A moment later Richard strode in carrying a loaded breakfast tray. He was wearing a short navy-blue silk robe and, apart from one dark lock that had escaped to fall over his forehead, his hair had been tamed into submission.

He looked clear-eyed and incredibly handsome and, though she tried her hardest to appear cool and composed, her heart picked up speed.

Studying her shiny nose and the damp strands of hair escaping from the clip, he commented gravely, 'You've had your shower, I see.'

Feeling a disturbing mixture of embarrassment and powerful attraction and knowing her hair must look ridiculous bundled on top of her head like this, she wished she'd had time to brush it.

'How's the ankle this morning?'

Somehow she found her voice and said huskily, 'Much better, thank you.'

Having set the tray on the bedside cabinet, he crossed to the window to draw back the curtains. 'We seem to have our good weather back,' he observed as the sunshine flooded in. 'Which should be a relief after yesterday.'

Almost to himself and with a little reminiscent smile, he added, 'However, rain like that can create some lasting memories…'

She was wondering what kind of memories he had in mind when, returning to the bedside, he stooped to touch his lips to hers before asking, 'Now, about ready for some breakfast?'

Quivering from that casual little caress, she trapped the duvet under her arms and looked anywhere but at him as he set the tray across her knees.

It held freshly squeezed grapefruit juice and a full English breakfast, including toast and marmalade and a pot of coffee.

'As I'm aiming for a black belt in cooking and I don't get a chance to practise while Gwen's here, I thought I might as well go the whole hog.

'But, first of all, drink this.' He handed her a glass containing a small amount of cloudy liquid.

Though the actual taste wasn't too bad, the concoction had an unpleasant slimy texture and she shuddered as she swallowed it.

'Pretty revolting, isn't it?' he commented cheerfully. 'But it's extremely effective; the best cure for a hangover I know. By the time you've had something to eat, your headache will be gone.'

He poured the coffee, which was hot and fragrant, and, having divided the sausages, bacon, button mushrooms and grilled tomatoes between two plates, paused to ask, 'Now, then, how brave do you feel?'

'Brave?'

He grinned. 'While everything else is usually eatable, my scrambled eggs have been known to resemble foam rubber, so it's up to you.'

Raising a well-marked brow, he added quizzically, 'Are you brave enough to try a spoonful?'

Suddenly *liking* him a lot, she smiled and nodded.

'Your courage is only exceeded by your personal beauty,' he told her and, having added the eggs, put a plate in front of her. 'There you are, tuck in. You'll feel a lot better when you've eaten.'

He took a napkin and his own plate and sat down companionably on the edge of the bed.

It was all so intimate they could have been lovers for years, she found herself thinking, or an old married couple.

But familiarity brought, if not contempt, a kind of serenity, and serenity was absent. His close proximity, her keen awareness of him, alerted all her senses and made her heart race and her temperature rise like a rocket.

Distracted, her appetite suddenly non-existent, she sipped her coffee and considered telling him that she wasn't hungry after all.

But, unwilling to hurt his feelings, she finally picked up her knife and fork and began to eat. After the first mouthful or two she found, unexpectedly, that her appetite had returned.

Somewhat to her surprise—most of the men she had known in the past could scarcely boil water—everything was cooked to perfection and the eggs proved to be deliciously light and fluffy.

But then he was the kind of man who would excel at anything he set his hand to.

Glancing up, she met his tawny eyes.

'Well?' he queried.

'You're awarded a black belt.'

'That's good.' With a small secret smile he added, 'It's my aim to please you in every way.'

That smile and the gleam in his eyes made her wonder if the innocent words had a double meaning and, feeling the colour rise in her cheeks, she hastily returned her attention to her meal.

He had put their empty plates on one side and offered her the toast rack before he broke the silence to ask, 'Feeling any better?'

Starting to butter her toast, she answered, 'Much better, thank you,' and was surprised to find it was the truth. Her headache had lifted and the feeling of nausea had vanished.

Smiling at her, he said, 'That's good.'

He had leaned forward to help himself to a piece of toast when, glancing up, she saw that a stray shaft of sunshine had fallen across his handsome face, lighting it up.

Fascinated, she stared into his eyes. The irises, dark green and ringed with gold, had flecks of hazel and gold swimming in their tawny depths.

It seemed an age before she could tear her gaze away and return to her toast.

As, somewhat distractedly, she finished spreading it, she got a smear of marmalade on the index finger of her left hand. She was about to lick if off when he lifted her hand and, putting her finger in his mouth, sucked.

Feeling the warmth and wetness, the slight roughness of his tongue, she caught her breath and her stomach tied itself in knots.

A moment later he released her hand and, as if nothing had happened, as if he hadn't shaken her to the very core, remarked, 'By the way, while breakfast was cooking I phoned the garage. I've made arrangements to have your car picked up and repaired as soon as possible.'

Her voice impeded, she said, 'Thank you. That's very kind of you.'

'It's the least I can do.'

'Perhaps if I give you my friend's address, you'll ask the garage to let me have the bill?'

Flatly, he said, 'I shall do no such thing. As I ran into you, the responsibility is mine... Now, then, more coffee?'

'Please.'

As he reached to replenish their coffee cups, his tone careless, he enquired, 'I take it you have no plans for the weekend?'

'I've trespassed long enough on your hospitality, so the first thing I must do is find a hotel...'

His mouth tightened. Once again she wasn't reacting as he might have expected and he couldn't afford to let her move into a hotel. While she was under his roof, he wanted to keep her there.

'Then I intend to visit some employment agencies,' she went on, determinedly, 'and see what kind of jobs are currently available...'

That was another thing he couldn't let her do.

'Surely there's no need to look for work immediately? Won't you be receiving some kind of redundancy payment?'

'I was given six months' salary, which is really very generous. But when my flat is finished the rent will go up considerably. And, apart from that, I have financial commitments that make it necessary to find another job without too much delay.'

That could well be to his advantage, he thought. And then, though he already knew, he asked, 'What exactly did your previous job entail?'

'Tying up with the buyer to gather data and taste as many of the new vintages as possible; describing and cataloguing the wines; sending out promotional leaflets; organising the various social occasions and parties that are part of a sales push and making sure we received maximum press coverage.'

'Sounds like a job and a half. But I gather you enjoyed it?'

She sighed. 'Yes, I did, very much. Losing it came as a blow.'

'It must have done.'

'What are the chances of joining another vintner?'

'Unfortunately, not very high, unless I was prepared to work abroad.'

'And you don't want to do that?'

'Not really.' She needed to be on hand to try and make sure that Didi didn't go off the rails again.

'But you'd prefer to be in the wine trade?'

'It's what I spent over three years studying for.'

'Three years?' He seemed surprised.

'I did one year at college and another two on the practical side.'

'Where did you get your hands-on experience?'

'I spent two years working at the Château de Renard, learning about soil composition, planting methods, culture and yields, what factors need to be present to produce a good vintage, how to most successfully blend the various grape types—'

She stopped speaking abruptly, wondering if she was boring him.

But, looking anything but bored, he exclaimed, 'Then you're just the woman I need!'

As she stared at him, he explained, 'You have exactly the kind of knowledge and experience that I've been hoping to find.

'Our family home is at Castle Anders…'

'Is Castle Anders the name of a place or is it a…?' She hesitated and broke off in confusion.

'A real castle?' he finished for her.

'Well, yes…' she said, flushing a little.

Looking amused, he told her, 'It's a real castle.'

So his family home was a castle!

Her heart sank. If, hating the thought of never seeing him again, she had harboured any faint hope of staying in his life, that killed it stone dead. With money and a privileged background like that, he was right out of her class.

'Though the estate is still extensive,' he went on, 'the castle itself is quite small as castles go. No larger, in fact, than, say, a reasonably sized hall, but with more turrets.

'But, to get back to the point, although Anders is only just over an hour's drive from London, we've a small vineyard on the estate.

'The winery hasn't been in production for quite a number of years but I've always had it in mind that if and when the opportunity arose I'd try and give it a new lease of life.'

Finding her voice, Tina hazarded, 'So you'd like some advice?'

'I was thinking of rather more than that. As your needs and my needs seem to coincide, I was offering you a job.'

'A job?'

By rights she should have been ecstatic, but now a miracle had happened she simply felt numb.

'You said you needed one,' he pointed out.

With no chance of any other relationship developing, working for him would be one way of staying in his life.

But wouldn't it be awkward and embarrassing, put her in an untenable position, to work for a man she had been to bed with?

'I do, but I…I really don't think…'

He had hoped for a more positive, a more favourable, response. But, wary of exerting too much pressure, he said easily, 'Well, you don't have to decide right this minute…

'Tell you what, I'll ask Jervis to bring the car round and as soon as you're up and dressed we'll go over to Anders. After you've seen the castle and the vineyard we can talk about it further.'

She had opened her mouth to refuse, when she hesitated. Though nothing could come of it, she found she badly wanted to spend a little more time with him, see his family home.

Watching her face, trying to gauge her reaction, he wondered how to play it. Would it be best to turn on the heat or allow her a breathing space?

But what if she decided against going to Anders? He couldn't afford to let her take the initiative and walk away. Somehow he had to make her *want* to stay with him.

His mind made up, he rose to his feet in a leisurely manner and, removing the tray, set it down on the Elizabethan blanket chest.

When he didn't immediately leave, unwilling to let him see her get out of bed naked, she stayed where she was until, with an innocent look, he queried, 'Something wrong?'

'My dressing gown's still in my case,' she explained awkwardly.

He crossed to where her case was and returned a moment later with her lightweight dressing gown over his arm. Instead of handing it to her, however, he stood by the bed and held it for her.

When still she hesitated, he said quizzically, 'Don't tell me you're shy, after last night?'

Watching her bite her lip, he laughed softly. 'Why, I do believe you are. But then if you remember how—'

'I'm afraid I don't remember much about it,' she broke in desperately.

'Much?'

'Anything,' she admitted.

'Ah,' he murmured softly. 'Well, if you'd like me to refresh your memory…?'

Thoroughly hot and bothered, her equilibrium gone, she exclaimed, 'No!' Then, less vehemently, 'No, I wouldn't…I mean I…I just want to get dressed.'

He frowned. Though she had been wrong-footed from the start, it was already clear that she had much more strength of character than he'd envisaged and he couldn't make up his mind whether, in the long run, that was a good thing or not.

But one thing he did know. While she was off balance it would pay him to *keep* her off balance…

With a sigh he said, 'Then perhaps I'd better stop teasing you.'

The mock contrition on his face and the devilish gleam in his eyes made him totally irresistible.

Realising that he had no real intention of stopping and knowing she would have to make a move or endure even more, she slid out of bed and, her back turned to him, slipped into the silky gown.

Wrapping it round her and holding it in place with his arms, he touched his lips to the warmth of her nape, planting soft little baby kisses until he reached the warm hollow behind her ear.

As, shivers running up and down her spine, she stood perfectly still, not daring to move, his mouth travelled down the side of her neck, nibbling and sucking, making her want to squirm.

At the same time his hands slid up to cup her breasts. Through the thin material of her gown, she could feel the warmth of his palms and her heart began to race madly. When his thumbs brushed over her sensitive nipples she gasped.

Part of her mind was aware that she ought to pull free, put a stop to this madness before she reached the point of no return.

But still she continued to stand rooted to the spot while his hands caressed her breasts, sending needle-sharp darts of pleasure running through her.

Just when she thought she could stand no more of such exquisite torment, he stopped and, turning her into his arms, lifted her chin and began to kiss her.

While she tried to hold on to the coat tails of her fast disappearing self-control and call a halt, he plundered her mouth with a masterful expertise that soon, caught in the spell of the black magic he was weaving, left her limp and quivering all over.

She had never known it could be like this. Had never imagined anyone being able to make her feel such longing, such naked need.

When finally he slipped the dressing gown from her shoulders and laid her down on the bed, mindless with desire, she made no demur.

For a brief moment he stood looking down at her, half regretting what he intended to do, wishing that circumstances were other than what they were.

Her flawless skin, her long slender limbs, her beautifully shaped breasts, her slim waist and flat stomach, the seductive curve of her hips, would have tempted the most dedicated of monks.

Tossing aside his own robe, he stretched out naked beside her and, murmuring how beautiful she was, began to kiss her again, expertly and thoroughly.

CHAPTER FOUR

WHILE he kissed her his skilful hands travelled caressingly over her body, filling her with a singing delight. A sensation that intensified almost unbearably as, his finger and thumb teasing one pink nipple, he took the other into his mouth and stroked it with the tip of his tongue.

While he continued to ravish her, his free hand began to explore the silky honey-gold triangle of curls and the satiny skin of her inner thighs.

She began to make soft little sounds deep in her throat, wordless pleas that he heard with a wholly masculine satisfaction.

But now was the time to make his move while he was still in control. If he left it any longer...

When, in response to her urging, he moved over her, after a lifetime of discipline and self-restraint it seemed the most natural thing in the world to welcome him and, feeling his weight, she gave a little murmur of pleasure.

A murmur that died in her throat as, all at once, muttering something she didn't catch, he drew away.

Her eyes flew open.

He got to his feet, pulled the duvet over her and shrugged into his robe while she lay there, bereft and bewildered.

Deplorably innocent she might be, but there wasn't the

faintest doubt that he'd wanted her, so what had made him change his mind so suddenly?

Bending down, he kissed her and said quietly, 'Gwen's back early…'

She hadn't heard a thing, Tina thought dazedly, but in the circumstances that wasn't surprising.

'There's no guarantee that she won't come upstairs,' he went on, 'and the guest room doesn't have a key, so to save everyone's blushes I'll take the evidence and make myself scarce.'

Picking up the tray, he headed for the door.

Watching it close behind him, it struck her that, far from being seriously annoyed, he seemed to be taking the whole thing in his stride.

Almost as if he had planned to walk away at that point…

But why on earth should he? It didn't make sense. She dismissed the ridiculous thought. It would simply be that what would have been new and earth-shaking for her wouldn't mean the same to him.

Though, judging by the care he had taken to avoid upsetting his housekeeper, he didn't bring his women here, he must be used to having his every need met. Which meant he could regard the interruption as just a slight annoyance.

Whereas she felt empty and desolate, like someone who had been torn from the gates of paradise just as they were about to open…

But, unless she wanted to risk Mrs Baxter finding her like this, she mustn't lie here repining.

The thought galvanizing her into action, she got out of bed and pulled on her gown while she found fresh underwear and a clean blouse.

While she had been drifting along, sexually unawakened, it had been comparatively easy to deny her body's needs. But being awakened, feeling really alive for the first time, though wonderful, was a two-edged sword.

Trying to ignore the way her body still cried out for fulfilment, the demons of frustration that clamoured for release, she put on her suit, coiled her hair and made-up lightly.

Then she repacked her case, gathered up her coat and handbag and, allowing herself no more time for regrets or thoughts of what might have been, made her way downstairs.

There was no sign of either the housekeeper or Richard and everything was quiet as she descended the stairs.

In the hall she hesitated, suddenly embarrassed at the thought of having to face him after everything that had happened.

It would be so much easier if she was free to just slip away, as self-sufficient, as *uninvolved* as she had been before she had first seen him standing in Cartel's car park.

But she wasn't.

No longer mistress of her own destiny, at this precise moment she could no more make herself walk away and leave him than she could fly to the moon. As though caught in a spell, she was held by invisible bonds, ties she didn't begin to understand but couldn't escape.

It was both a frightening and strangely exhilarating thought.

She couldn't be in love. It couldn't have happened this fast. But from being a woman very much alone, trapped in an emotional vacuum, overnight everything had changed. She had finally been awakened and was alive in a way that she had never known before.

Even when she and Kevin had been newly engaged and she had thought she loved him, she had never felt like this.

But, no matter how she felt, when they got back from Castle Anders, for the sake of her self-respect, she must move into a hotel.

Leaving her case in the hall, she headed for the study. As she reached the door she heard Richard's voice and hesitated.

'Yes, I'm sorry about that, but as things are…' he was saying. Then, after a pause, 'I have to act now…I simply can't afford to risk waiting…'

She had started to turn away as, his voice brisk and determined, he went on, 'I certainly hope so… Straight away, all being well… Now, I'd better get moving… Yes, I'll do that… Bye.'

The door opened abruptly and he came striding out. His dark face more than a little tense, he said, 'I was just coming to look for you. About ready to go?'

'Yes.' Whatever the trip to Castle Anders brought, it was something she felt impelled to do.

His face relaxing into a smile, he said, 'That's good,' and put a hand at her waist.

Just that light touch seemed to brand her through her clothing.

'As it's a Saturday morning and the traffic's often bad,' he went on, 'it might take us longer than usual to get there. But we can always have lunch on the way—' Seeing her case, he stopped speaking abruptly.

Quickly, before she could weaken, she explained, 'I've brought my belongings in the hope that when we get back to London you'll be kind enough to drop me at a hotel.'

'Of course,' he agreed smoothly, 'if you're sure that's what you want.'

Outside, the sky was a Mediterranean blue and it was warm and sunny, with a return to the Indian summer they had been enjoying. A balmy breeze carried the scent of late roses and somewhere close at hand a bird sang, turning town into country.

The sleek silver Porsche was standing by the kerb with a dark blue limousine drawn up behind it and Jervis—stocky and middle-aged—standing by.

Handing the chauffeur Tina's case, Richard said, 'I've decided to drive myself, so you can put that in the Porsche, garage the limo and take the rest of the day off.'

'Very good, sir.' There was gladness and relief in the man's voice. 'Thank you, sir.'

'I suppose you know your favourite team's on the box this afternoon?' Richard queried with a grin.

Jervis returned the grin. 'Don't I just! And they stand a good chance of winning.

'There's a special preview before the run-up to the match,' he went on, 'so as soon as Mrs Baxter gets back—they're her favourite team too—we'll have an early lunch and get settled.'

So the housekeeper *wasn't* back. Richard must have been mistaken. *Or lying deliberately.*

Oh, don't start that again! Tina scolded herself and wondered what had got into her. Usually she was well-balanced, not one to harbour foolish thoughts, but somehow, since yesterday lunch time, she had lost her common sense along with her equilibrium.

As soon as her case was in the boot and she was installed in the passenger seat, with a word of thanks and a nod to the chauffeur, Richard slid in beside her. A moment later they had left the quiet square and joined the busy Saturday morning mêlée.

As they headed out of town, the traffic proved to be very heavy and it was stop-start for most of the way. Once the suburbs had been left behind them, however, and they reached the quieter country roads, things improved enormously.

When it was obvious that the most stressful part of the journey was over, she asked, 'Where exactly is Castle Anders?'

'Some five miles from the picturesque market town of Anders Cross and a couple of miles from the village of West Anders.'

It seemed that Anders was a name to be reckoned with, Tina thought a shade dazedly and asked, 'How long have the Anders family lived there?'

'Our branch of the family have lived at the castle for well over six hundred years.'

She was still marvelling at that when he went on, 'My mother, who lost both her parents in a plane crash when she was just a toddler, was brought up there by her grandparents.

'When she met and fell in love with my father, Richard Cavendish, and wanted to marry him, they gave the couple their blessing on condition that he changed his name from Cavendish to Anders and made his home at the castle. Which he did.

'When my great-grandfather passed away at ninety-three, he left me his business empire and bequeathed Castle Anders to my mother on the understanding that after her death it should come to me…'

'So your parents still live there?'

He shook his head. 'They're both dead.' Heavily, he added, 'My mother died earlier this year.'

'I'm sorry,' she said. 'You must miss her.'

He acknowledged her condolence with a glance from those tawny eyes and a little nod.

'Have you any brothers or sisters?'

'No. I'm the last of this particular branch of the family—at least until I marry and have children of my own.

'Then, as great-grandfather knew, it's always been my intention to take my wife and family and live at Anders on a permanent basis.'

Tina felt a queer tug at her heartstrings to think that some lucky woman was destined to be everything to him—his friend and confidante, his lover and his wife, the mother of his children.

Trying to push the poignant thought aside, she relapsed into silence and stared out at the scenery. Without being particularly dramatic, the countryside was pleasantly picturesque and rolling.

The woods were decked in bronze and gold and russet, the newly washed meadows were green and lush and the silver flash of water told of quiet streams and rivers.

As they breasted a rise to see a pleasing panorama spread out below them, Richard broke the silence to say, 'A mile or so ahead, there's a nice old coaching inn called the Posthorn. I thought we might stop there. The place has character and the food's good.'

She nodded agreement. 'That sounds lovely.'

The Posthorn was a black and white half-timbered place with tubs of trailing scarlet geraniums adding a vivid splash of colour.

Richard drove through an archway into a cobbled yard and parked outside what had obviously once been stabling and now appeared to be a small brewery.

'As you can see, they brew their own ale here,' he remarked, 'and it's excellent.'

They went in through a back door and into a panelled lounge, where the windows were open to the balmy air and sunshine streamed in.

In the huge fireplace the grate was screened by a large jar filled with beech and autumn foliage and the polished furniture smelt of apples and honey.

Having settled her in a seat by a window, he handed her a menu and asked, 'What do you fancy to eat?'

'I'm not particularly hungry after such a good breakfast…' she began and, recalling the intimacy of that breakfast, felt her cheeks grow hot.

Seeing the gleam of amusement in his eyes and knowing he'd guessed the cause of her confusion, she found herself blushing even harder.

His face straight, he suggested, 'Then perhaps just a sandwich?'

Not knowing where to look, she bent her head over the menu and studied it with unnecessary care.

Oh, why was she acting like an overgrown schoolgirl? she wondered crossly. Where had yesterday's cool, self-contained young woman gone?

But, after all that had happened last night and this morning… She pushed away the uncomfortable thought, determined not to go along *that* route, and dragged her mind back to the present.

There was an extensive range of light snacks and, by the time a cheerful buxom woman came to take their order, Tina had decided on home-cooked ham in a piece of French stick and a side salad.

Richard followed suit.

'And to drink?' he queried. Adding, 'They have a good wine cellar here.'

'I was thinking of trying half a pint of ale.'

Looking surprised, he said, 'A good choice. I'll have the same.'

Their ale came almost at once and, when she had sampled it and agreed that it was some of the best she'd ever tasted, he said, 'Tell me a bit about yourself. Are you London born and bred?'

'No. I was born and brought up in a small village. I only went to live in London when I started to work for Cartel Wines.'

'So which do you prefer? Town or country?'

She smiled wistfully. 'I quite like London but I'd much sooner live in the country.'

'Have you any brothers or sisters?'

'I've a stepsister, Didi. My mother died when I was seven and a year later my father married a widow with a daughter of almost the same age.'

'Did you get on well?'

'Not too well,' Tina admitted. 'Despite the fact that we were born in the same month and within three days of each other, we were completely different both in character and temperament.'

'Does your stepsister still live in the country?'

Tina shook her head. 'No. Didi left home and got a job in London when she was seventeen.'

'What about your parents?'

'A couple of years ago a relative left my father a hotel in Melbourne and they decided to give up their house and go to live in Australia.

'Before they went, they asked me to keep an eye on Didi—she'd been ill and was having problems.

'By that time I was working for Cartel Wines and renting a two-bedroomed flat, so when I found she couldn't pay the rent for her crummy bedsit and was about to be thrown out, I persuaded her to move in with me.'

Frowning, he asked, 'But she doesn't still live with you?'

'Oh, no. She moved out when she was offered a place at the Ramon Bonaventure School of Drama.'

'She wants to be an actress?'

'Yes. Though her mother had been very much against it, it was something Didi had always hoped to do…'

Tina stopped speaking as their lunch arrived, accompanied by various jars of homemade chutney, all with frilled muslin covers.

'I can thoroughly recommend the mango,' Richard told her.

'Mmm,' Tina agreed when she'd tried some. 'It's absolutely delicious.'

'I thought you'd like it. It's almost as good as Hannah makes.'

'Hannah?'

'Our old cook/housekeeper at the castle. Her family have been retainers there for donkey's years. Though Hannah's semi-retired, she still rules the staff with a rod of iron.

'She was born there and stayed on when she married one of the estate workers. Mullins, her son, is a general manservant who takes care of just about everything, including the cars, and her youngest granddaughter, Milly, is a maid.'

For a while they ate without speaking and, though Tina strove to appear relaxed and easy, she was *aware* of him—of his presence, his nearness, his every slight movement.

From beneath her thick lashes she watched him as he helped himself to more chutney and lifted his glass to drink. He had strong, well-shaped hands with lean fingers and neatly trimmed nails.

Masculine hands.

Exciting hands.

A half-remembered line from Donne started to run through her mind: *'Licence my roving hands, and let them go—'*

She snapped off the thought like snapping a dry twig and, feeling the sexual tension tightening, hurried into speech. 'How did the castle come to have a vineyard?'

'While my great-grandfather, who was a merchant banker,

was staying in a French château in the Loire Valley, he became very interested in wine-making. When he got back to Anders, he planted vines on some south-facing slopes on the edge of the estate and set up a small winery.

'By the time he passed away he had quite a successful little business which eventually my father took over. But when *he* became ill it was neglected and after his death I regret to say that it was closed down altogether.

'I was at Oxford at the time and after I graduated, though my mother begged me to go back to live at Anders, I decided, in the end, not to.'

'So you prefer to live in London?'

'No, not at all. Though I've lived in London since I left university, it isn't really from choice.'

'Oh.'

'My father died when I was eighteen and two years later my mother married again. She and my father had been very close and it was when she was alone and grief-stricken that she met Bradley Sanderson, a childless widower fifteen years older than herself.'

Seeing Tina's slightly puzzled frown, Richard explained, 'My mother decided that she would keep her own name. It seemed like the simplest solution—there is always meant to be an Anders in the castle. Though they had the same surname, he wasn't a blood relation. When he was five or six he'd been adopted by Jonathan Anders, a member of the Wiltshire branch of the family, whose wife was unable to have children.

'Unfortunately Bradley and I didn't get along. I disliked and distrusted him and he hated my guts for opposing the marriage.

'That's why, after leaving university, I decided it would be better all round if I lived in London. So I bought the house in Pemberley Square and just paid periodic visits to the castle, where I had my own suite of rooms.'

It must have been hard to visit a place he'd always regarded as home and confine himself to a suite of rooms, while a man he disliked intensely was, nominally at least, master there.

Impulsively, she said, 'It couldn't have been easy for you.'

For a moment he looked surprised, then he admitted, 'It wasn't. Especially when I realised Mother wasn't very happy…

'To give Bradley his due, he did a good job of running the estate and she was grateful. But he turned out to be a difficult man to live with and, though she never admitted as much, I think she regretted marrying him, and felt guilty that she *did* regret it.

'Shortly after she had been diagnosed with a terminal illness, Bradley was found to have a heart disease which cut his life expectancy to a year or two at the most.

'I promised Mother that if she predeceased him, I wouldn't turn him out. But he wasn't happy with that assurance. He wanted her to put a codicil in her will to the effect that he could continue to live at Anders until his death, and I agreed.'

'Then your stepfather's still living there?'

'He was until he died of a heart attack a little while ago.'

'So now the castle's all yours and you intend to keep it?'

Richard's handsome face looked oddly grim and his voice was steely as he answered, 'Oh, yes, I intend to keep it.'

The casement clock in the corner struck a sonorous two-thirty and, his voice and manner back to normal, Richard asked, 'About ready to move?'

Realising that at the rate they were going it would be quite late by the time they got back to London, she said, 'Yes, I'm ready,' and rose to her feet.

Apart from some brief embarrassment, it had been a very pleasant interlude and she had learned quite a lot about him and his family.

None of it had given her any hope that she might be lucky enough to fit into his life, but even so, knowing more about him, getting to understand him, was oddly precious to her.

While they continued their journey she mulled over what she

had learned and was still thinking about it when Richard said with satisfaction, 'Almost there.'

A minute or so later they left a quiet country road for an even quieter lane, with open countryside on their right and a high mellow-brick wall on their left. In a few hundred yards they came to an imposing entrance guarded by two huge stone lions crouched on stone plinths.

As they swung between them, the tall electronically operated wrought iron gates slid aside and a moment later the Porsche was purring up a well-kept serpentine drive. On either hand, rolling, lightly wooded parkland studded with sheep stretched away into the distance.

'Time's getting on, so I suggest that before I show you the castle we take a quick look at the vineyard,' Richard said.

She nodded. 'Whatever suits you best.'

Having agreed to come with him, she could hardly refuse to look at the vineyard. Besides, rather against her will, she was interested. If things had been different, the job would have been ideal.

After about three quarters of a mile they turned down a side road and eventually came to a collection of purpose-built sheds and buildings that housed the wine-making plant. On the nearby south-facing slopes stretched row upon row of vines.

Having stopped the car, he asked, 'Ankle up to a little walking?'

'Yes, certainly.'

He came round to help her out and, with an intimate little gesture that made her catch her breath, reached for her hand and tucked it under his arm.

Though the sun was still shining, the air seemed appreciably cooler and a slight breeze had sprung up as they strolled through what had once been a thriving little vineyard.

Now the vines were overgrown and neglected and, through the grass and weeds that partially obscured them, Tina could see purple grapes hanging in great heavy clusters.

'I presume that a lot of these vines will have to come out?' Richard enquired.

'Not necessarily if they're healthy stock. Though some re-planting might be advisable, depending on what kind of wine you're hoping to produce.'

'I see... Well, I suggest that we discuss the whole thing later when you've had time to consider exactly what's involved.'

'I really don't think there's any point in—'

He pre-empted her refusal. 'Unless, having seen how badly neglected everything's been, you don't feel you want to take it on?'

She shook her head. 'No, it isn't that.' It was exactly the kind of challenge she would enjoy. Or *would have* enjoyed had the circumstances been other than they were.

'Then what is it?'

'I would have liked the job, but...'

'But?'

'In the circumstances, it w-would be awkward,' she stammered.

'You mean after last night?'

Her silence was answer enough.

Once again she wasn't acting as he might have expected but, as he'd only used the job offer as a ploy to get her to the castle, it didn't much matter if she did refuse it.

She was here, out of harm's way, so to speak, and here he intended her to stay just in case they tried to make contact by phone.

Following that train of thought, he frowned. They wouldn't be able to reach her at Cartel Wines—he'd seen to that—but if they tried to contact her at home, the friend she was staying with would no doubt be able to give them her mobile number...

Which, come Monday, could pose a problem if he didn't do something about it...

As the silence lengthened uncomfortably, she glanced at him and, seeing the grim look on his face, said unhappily, 'I'm sorry...'

Collecting himself, he smiled down at her reassuringly. 'Don't worry about it… Let's go on up to the castle, shall we?'

They had returned to the main drive and followed it for perhaps half a mile when, at the end of a narrow track to the left, she saw part of a ruined tower built on a mound.

'That's Daland Tower,' Richard told her. 'All that's still standing of the original eleventh-century castle. Anders is a few hundred yards to the east. There, it's just coming into view…'

She caught a brief glimpse of grey walls and battlements but, before she could take any of it in, it had vanished from view behind a stand of tall trees decked in their autumn livery.

It wasn't until after they had climbed a little more and rounded the next bend that Richard stopped the car and she saw it clearly.

She caught her breath.

Small it might be, a castle in miniature, but it was a perfect little gem. Serene and enchanted, its grey towers and turrets etched against the deep blue of the sky, it was like something out of a fairy tale.

When, wholly entranced, she had gazed her fill, she turned shining eyes on her companion, who had been sitting quietly watching her reaction, and breathed, 'I'm not surprised you love it. It's wonderful.'

Her enthusiasm was so genuine, so spontaneous, that he found himself with very mixed feelings.

'Of course an old pile like this has its drawbacks,' he said carefully, 'and, though over the years parts of it have been modernized to make it more liveable in, structurally it's the same…

'Which means it needs a great deal of maintenance and takes almost every penny the estate makes to keep it in good order.'

Turning her head to smile at him, she said dreamily, 'But it must be well worth it to have a place like this.'

Throwing in his hand, he admitted, 'I think so.'

Her eyes turned once more to the castle and, watching her

glowing face, he thought she looked like a child gazing at something rare and magical.

He felt a strange pang. If only she hadn't been who she was; if only she had been as sweet and innocent as she appeared. But she was, and she wasn't.

After a few moments, as she continued to gaze, enraptured, he started the car and drove on.

As they passed a track to the right, he told her, 'Down there, beyond the back entrance, is the old stabling and coach house, the orangery, the herb garden and the kitchen gardens…'

Half hidden behind the towering grey walls of the castle, Tina could make out a sizable area of outbuildings and glasshouses.

'Apart from a couple of stalls that are in use,' Richard went on, 'the stabling has been converted into garages.'

'So you still have horses?'

'Two. Jupiter and Juno. Though Bradley disliked horses and wanted Mother to get rid of them both, she refused to part with them.

'Until she got too ill to ride, on my visits home I used to go out with her. Do you ride?'

'I used to love to. Though it's been years since I was on a horse.'

They were nearing the castle now and, craning her neck, she cried excitedly, 'Oh, there's a moat…'

'Yes and quite a deep one. But where, in the past, it was one of the castle's main defences, these days it's simply home to a variety of ducks and carp.

'It's fed by an underground stream. The same stream supplied the household wells and, because of its pureness, kept the inhabitants free from the diseases caused by contaminated water.'

As they drew nearer she exclaimed, 'And what a lovely old bridge…'

In truth it was a picture, its lichen-covered stones draped with delicate trails of small-leafed creeper spangled with tiny mauve and white flowers.

'This bridge wasn't built until about a hundred and fifty years ago,' he told her as they drove across it and through an archway into a cobbled courtyard. 'Before that there was a wooden drawbridge and a portcullis.'

His voice holding a hint of derision, he added, 'Now it's your turn to cry, "How romantic!"'

Flushing a little, she said quietly, 'I'm sorry. Did I go over the top?'

Feeling ashamed, he brought the car to a halt in front of an imposing oak door and, taking her hand, raised it to his lips. 'No, I'm the one who should be sorry. I'm just being a bear. As a matter of fact it's nice to find someone genuinely enthusiastic about the old place.'

Despite his apology she still looked uncomfortable and, watching her half-averted face, he cursed himself for the way he had lashed out at her simply because she liked it.

For one thing, none of this mess was her fault and, for another, if he lost ground it could easily wreck all his plans.

Bearing that in mind, he released the hand he was still holding, then turned to unfasten both their seat belts.

He was so close she could feel his breath on her cheek and she sat still as any statue.

When she continued to look straight ahead, using a single finger he turned her face to his.

'Forgive me?'

'There's nothing to forgive.'

'Kind and generous as well as beautiful,' he murmured softly.

His mouth was only inches from hers and she froze.

Afraid he was going to kiss her.

Afraid he wasn't.

His kiss, when it came, was as light as thistledown, but it scattered her wits, brought every nerve-ending in her body zinging into life and effortlessly rekindled that morning's burning desire. As her lips quivered beneath his, he ran the tip of his tongue between them, finding the silky, sensitive inner skin, teasing and tantalizing, coaxing them to part.

When they did, he deepened the kiss until her head reeled and, caught in a spell of sensual delight, she lost all sense of time and place.

Slipping his hand inside her jacket, he brushed his fingertips lightly over her breasts and, feeling the nipples firm beneath his touch, smiled to himself. She was obviously a passionate woman and quick to respond, as he'd discovered that morning.

The only problem was that in deliberately arousing her he'd been hoist with his own petard and had felt as frustrated as hell ever since.

But now wasn't the time to take her to bed, he reminded himself, there were still things to do, things to be settled. There would be time for pleasure when everything was going smoothly.

CHAPTER FIVE

DRAWING away with reluctance, Richard said, 'We'd better go in before Hannah, who never misses a thing though she's nearly eighty, comes out to see what could be keeping us.'

As he spoke, one leaf of the heavy studded door opened and a small woman, hardly bigger than a child, with a silver bun and a very straight back, appeared.

'What did I tell you?' he murmured, and left the car to come round and help Tina out.

In something of a daze, she picked up her shoulder bag and allowed herself to be led across the cobbles to where the old woman waited.

As they approached, the housekeeper, who was neatly dressed in old-fashioned black and wore a jet necklace and earrings, came forward to meet them.

'Mr Richard…' Her wizened face creased into a beam of pleasure. 'Welcome home! Everything's ready for you.

'It seems to have turned a shade cooler and, as I know how much you like a good fire, I've had one lit in the living-room.' Then, with genuine emotion, 'It's nice to have you back.'

'It's nice to be back, Hannah.' His arm around Tina's shoulders, he added, 'This is the lady I told you about when I rang.'

Shrewd dark eyes, bright as a bird's, acknowledged Tina's smile and weighed her up. Then, apparently satisfied with what she saw, the housekeeper's face relaxed into a smile. 'It's a pleasure to meet you, Miss Dunbar. If you need a ladies' maid, please let me know.'

Hannah appeared to think they were staying and, before Richard could put her right, she went on, 'I've ordered roast pheasant for dinner, which cook's timing for seven-thirty if that suits you? But the kettle's just boiled if you'd like a cup of tea in the meantime?'

'We'd love one,' he told her. 'But get young Milly to do the running about.'

'I must admit that these days I'm glad to,' Hannah confessed. 'Though I keep very well, thank the good Lord, I'm not as nimble on my feet as I used to be.'

But, as though to disprove those words, she led the way into the hall in a sprightly fashion and disappeared through a small door at the rear.

The panelled hall, with its black oak floorboards and huge stone fireplace, was furnished with lovingly polished antiques and lit by long, intricately leaded windows that bore the maker's name and the date. On the right, an elegant oak staircase with a lion's head on the newel post climbed to a small minstrels' gallery.

Tina thought it was absolutely beautiful, but hesitated to say so. Even when Richard gave her an interrogative glance, she refrained from comment.

He turned to face her and, putting a hand against her cheek in an oddly remorseful gesture, remarked quietly, 'I'm sorry. It wasn't my intention to spoil it for you.'

Finding her voice, she said, 'You haven't. I'm enjoying it all very much.'

'But afraid to say so?'

'A little wary,' she admitted.

'Please don't be.' He bent his head and kissed her lightly on the lips, making her pulses leap, before going on, 'These rooms off the hall form the main living area. The breakfast room, the morning room, the formal dining-room…' As he spoke he led her round the hall, opening doors to show glimpses of beautiful old rooms with wood-panelled walls and period furniture.

'The library-cum-study,' he went on, 'is the only room where the twenty-first century has been allowed to hold unreserved sway…'

Glancing in, Tina saw a pleasant room with book-lined walls and an oak-panelled ceiling. Ranged on an impressive leather-topped desk was a businesslike computer and an array of up-to-date communication equipment.

'And next door is the living-room…' A hand at her waist, he led her into a beautifully proportioned room with panelled walls and a white ceiling. Once again the leaded windows that looked across the courtyard were a work of art executed and signed by a master craftsman.

Most of the furniture was antique and bore the glorious patina of age, but the soft natural leather suite grouped around the inglenook fireplace was up-to-date and comfortable-looking.

A log fire blazed cheerfully in the grate, a grandfather clock tick-tocked in the corner and flowers and photographs made the room feel lived-in and homely.

This time Tina said without hesitation, 'What a lovely room.'

He gave her the kind of smile that made her heart turn over. 'I'm glad you like it.'

'And not a television in sight,' she added quizzically, remembering the comments he'd made the previous evening.

His smile widened into a grin. 'It wasn't easy to bring in modern technology without spoiling the atmosphere. But *voilà*!'

Sliding aside the doors of a large and handsome oak cabinet, he revealed a state-of-the-art television, a video, a DVD player and a comprehensive music centre.

'All the trappings of modern-day entertainment,' he said a shade wryly, 'though blessedly not on view unless they're in use.'

They had just settled themselves by the fireside when there

was a tap at the door and a young maid brought in a tray of tea and cake.

'Thanks, Milly,' Richard said. Adding, 'We'll pour our own.'

While Tina sat in front of the fire, he helped her to tea in a delicate china cup and a slice of homemade fruit cake, before sitting down opposite.

Though the setting seemed relaxed and homely, the silence companionable, there was still an undercurrent of sexual tension that rasped along her nerves like rough silk and, as she sipped her tea, she watched him surreptitiously.

Leaning back, his long legs stretched towards the hearth, he looked completely at his ease and she envied his cool detachment.

Glancing up, he caught her eye.

Her colour rising, she looked hastily away.

Hiding a smile, he said conversationally, 'Tell me something; if you had no intention of taking the job, why did you agree to come'?'

Her flush deepening, she confessed, 'I wanted to see the castle.'

'Ah,' he murmured softly.

'I'm sorry. I suppose it was a waste of your time.'

'Not at all,' he denied. 'I've enjoyed the day.'

'So have I,' she admitted. Then, reminding herself that it was something she *had* to do, she added, 'But I really ought to be getting back before too long. I've still got to find a hotel.'

Softly he said, 'After last night I was rather hoping you'd change your mind and stay with me.'

'Last night was a mistake,' she told him jerkily. 'If I hadn't had too much to drink…'

'And this morning?'

'That was a mistake too,' she insisted. 'I should never have let it happen.'

She sounded as if she meant it and he sighed inwardly. So much for trying to make sure she stayed. He could swear she still wanted him, but for some reason she was now playing hard to get.

He wondered why she was bothering. Was it possible that she was hoping for more than just an affair? Hoping to make him keen enough to get seriously involved?

In the past he'd frequently been the target for gold-diggers and women who were trying to land a rich husband, though usually they had gone about it in a different way.

However, if that *was* her aim and he moved with care, it could fit in nicely with his own plans.

The only thing he couldn't allow her was time…

When he remained silent, angry with herself for being weak enough to come, she said, 'If you were intending to stay here, as your housekeeper seems to think, I can always get a taxi back.'

It would cost a fortune but, having got herself into this mess…

'My dear Valentina,' he drawled, 'I haven't the slightest intention of allowing you to get a taxi. If you insist on going back, I'll take you myself.'

Uncomfortably, she said, 'Well, if you're sure you don't mind?'

'Of course I don't mind. I'm at your disposal. But, as you came to see the castle, it would be a shame to start back without taking a look at it, so I suggest a guided tour of the place and then dinner before we think of leaving. What do you say?'

There was only one thing she could say, and she said it. 'Thank you very much—that sounds lovely.'

'Sure your ankle will stand it?'

'Quite sure.'

'Then let's go.'

Leaving her bag where it was, she accompanied him across the hall and along a wide stone corridor.

'It's beginning to get dusk,' he remarked, 'so I suggest that, before we start the tour proper, we go up to the gatehouse, where there's a nice view across the park to the oval lake.'

As they began to climb the spiralling stone stairway, lit by candle bulbs in metal sconces, the air coming through the embrasures felt distinctly fresh and she half wished she had her coat, which she'd left in the car along with her case.

She found the gatehouse, with its huge stone fireplace and garderobe, fascinating, and lingered there for a while imagining what it must have been like when it was occupied. Only the realisation that time was flying and there was lots more to see made her move on.

Another flight of stone steps brought them to a small, thick, studded door, from which they emerged on to the roof of the gatehouse.

Tina glanced down into the courtyard, with its huge central well, now covered with a latticework of heavy metal, and, noticing that the Porsche was no longer there, remarked, 'Your car's gone.'

His voice casual, Richard said, 'Mullins must have presumed we were staying and put it away.'

Then, seeing she looked uneasy, 'Don't let it worry you; it's no major problem. After dinner, when we're ready to go, I can ask for it to be brought round. Now, come and look at the view.'

Hung with blue veils of twilight, the view across the rolling park to the faintly shimmering oval of the lake, the darkening woods and, closer at hand, Daland Tower, was beautiful.

One arm lightly around her shoulders, he pointed a steady finger. 'Over there, through a gap in the trees, you can just catch a glimpse of the lights of Farrington Hall. The O'Connells, who live there, are our nearest neighbours.'

The name *O'Connell* seemed oddly familiar, but it was a moment or two before Tina recalled that it had been a Helen O'Connell who had been trying to phone Richard the previous day.

It was a lovely evening and above the western horizon, where a pinky-gold afterglow was fading into greeny-blue, a single bright star shone.

Half under her breath, she murmured the jingle she remembered from childhood, 'Starlight, star bright, first star I've seen tonight...'

'The evening star,' Richard said. 'Are you going to wish on it?'

'Why not?' she agreed lightly. 'Though I fear my wish might be unattainable.'

'So might mine. But nothing ventured nothing gained, so let's give it a try.'

Folding his arms around her, he drew her back against his hard, muscular body and held her there. Then, bending his head so that his cheek touched hers, he urged, 'Wish away.'

Knees turned to water by his nearness, and only too aware that she might as well wish for the moon, she looked up at the glittering star and silently wished that one day Richard might come to care for her.

After a little while when, rooted to the spot by the feel of his slightly roughened cheek against hers, she continued to stand quite still, he debated whether to make his move now.

Deciding the time wasn't right, he straightened and said prosaically, 'We'd better get on with the tour, otherwise we'll be late for dinner.'

Like someone in a dream, she turned to walk back the way they had come.

'Careful on the stairs,' he warned and, an arm at her waist, guided her somewhat uncertain steps back down the stone stairway and thence to the passageway, to begin their tour proper.

Her first impression on seeing Anders had been that it was a gem of a place and that was amply confirmed as he showed her over it.

A picturesque castle with towers and turrets, secret passages and deep cellars, its own serenely beautiful little chapel with a resident priest, it was something very special. The fact that it was also a home made it rare indeed.

As they returned to the hall, glancing at his watch, Richard suggested, 'If you'd like to freshen up before dinner…?'

'Oh, yes, please.'

Having escorted her up the main staircase and past the minstrels' gallery, he opened a door on the right and ushered her inside a spacious suite, with a bedroom and bathroom either side of a central sitting-room.

'This suite was used by my parents when my father was alive,' he told her. 'My mother had this room as a den, to "sit and cogitate" as she put it, and deal with her correspondence.

'That's her escritoire.' He pointed to a small, exquisitely proportioned writing desk. 'It was made in the reign of Queen Anne.'

'It's absolutely beautiful,' Tina said, coming to take a closer look.

'My mother loved it. Apparently as a child she was fascinated by the fact that it has a secret drawer.

'When she came of age, her grandmother gave it to her as a twenty-first birthday present and she used it for the rest of her life.

'After my father died, and Mother remarried, these rooms were kept for my use when I visited the castle. Though Mother continued to use the sitting-room…

'This is the master bedroom…'

The master bedroom—simple yet grand, with its panelled walls and polished oak floorboards—had fine furniture and a handsomely carved four-poster bed with a scarlet and gold canopy.

'And this is the guest room…'

The guest room was equally spacious and beautiful, with period furniture and a four-poster bed with a dark blue tester.

One of the first things Tina noticed was that her coat and case had been brought up and placed on a low blanket chest.

Though Richard must have noticed it too, he made no comment. He merely went on, 'At one time this room was used as a dressing room. It was Mother's idea to make it into a guest bedroom, in case I wanted to bring a friend. Though I never did,' he added wryly.

Indicating the guest bathroom, he asked, 'How long do you need? Will fifteen minutes be enough?'

'Ample, thank you.'

'Then I'll have a quick shower and shave and wait for you in the hall.' He turned away.

Remembering the intimacy of that morning, she felt a queer sense of loss and disappointment. But she recognised that it was *her* attitude that was responsible for the change in him. *She* had altered things by her refusal to get involved any further.

Biting her lip, she went into an ivory and peach tiled bathroom which was not only well-equipped but sumptuous in the extreme, with a shelf full of luxurious toiletries, a couple of towelling robes and a pile of big soft towels.

It was in marked contrast to the bathroom in Ruth's bedsit, which was small and dingy, with a rusty boiler, a cracked sink and a shower stall that leaked.

When Tina had finished showering and dried herself, she wondered whether or not to change. Perhaps Richard wouldn't bother as they were going straight back to London after they'd eaten?

But a suit and flat-heeled shoes seemed all wrong for dining in a castle, and as her case was handy...

After a quick sort through what few clothes she had brought, she decided on a silky dress the purply-blue of heliotrope and, her ankle having so far stood the strain, a pair of high-heeled court shoes.

As she stood in front of an elegant cheval-glass to brush and re-coil her hair, she saw the four-poster reflected in it and imagined her friend's reaction to a bedroom like this.

Thinking about Ruth, it struck Tina what a lot she would have to tell her on Monday.

Only there were some things she couldn't even tell Ruth. Things that were far too intimate, far too precious, to talk about to anyone.

Sighing, she gazed into the mirror. Her eyes looked big and dark with secrets, her cheeks and lips a little pale.

With eyebrows and lashes that were naturally several shades

darker than her hair, she didn't need mascara, but some blusher and a touch of lip gloss would improve things enormously.

Her small cosmetic case was in her bag and she toyed with the idea of slipping downstairs to fetch it, before deciding there wasn't really time.

Ready to go down, she debated whether or not to take her coat and case with her. But in the end she put her coat over her arm and left her case where it was. No doubt Richard would ask whoever had taken it up to fetch it down again.

Though she was in good time, as she descended the stairs she saw that he was waiting for her in the hall. He had not only showered and shaved but had changed into a well-cut dinner jacket.

He looked heart-stoppingly virile and handsome and she felt all quivery inside to think what might have happened if, rather than going back to London, she'd been staying here.

But she *wasn't* staying, she reminded herself sharply. As soon as dinner was over they were leaving for town.

Stepping forward, he took her hand. 'You look delightful. That colour exactly matches your eyes.'

A shade awkwardly, she said, 'I wasn't sure whether you'd bother changing.'

Relieving her of her coat, he put it over a dark oak settle and tucked her hand through his arm. 'Given the circumstances, I wouldn't, only Mullins had laid everything out ready for me and I didn't want to hurt his feelings.

'Now, how about a pre-dinner drink in the study?'

'A drink?' She sounded as horrified as she felt.

Glancing at her, he burst out laughing.

He had a nice laugh, deep and infectious. 'If you could see your face!' Still smiling, he went on, 'I don't blame you for being wary, but I promise I was going to suggest something innocuous. A small sherry at the most. Nothing that would induce a hangover.'

'Thank heaven for that,' she said with feeling. And thought that with his tawny eyes still gleaming with amusement and his lean cheeks creased with laughter lines, he was totally irresistible.

He led her to the library-cum-study, where a cheerful log fire burnt in the grate and a drinks trolley waited.

'So what's it to be?'

Taking a seat by the fire, she said, 'I'll have that small sherry, please.'

'Cream or dry?'

'Dry.'

When he'd handed her a glass he sat down opposite and smiled at her.

'Aren't you having a drink?'

'As I'll be driving shortly, I'd better stick to a glass of wine with the meal.'

'I'm sorry,' she said. 'I feel guilty.'

'There's really no need. You made it clear from the start that you intended to go back to town and book into a hotel. I was just hoping that when you saw Anders you might change your mind.

'If you don't like the idea of sharing my bed,' he went on, 'you could always sleep in solitary state in the guest room.'

She was sorely tempted. But if she agreed to stay and he turned on the heat, could she trust herself to hold out against him?

As he waited for her answer, he decided that if this gamble didn't come off he would have to use delaying tactics until he found some other way to keep her here. *Without rousing her suspicions.*

When still she hesitated he asked, 'Have you ever slept in a four-poster bed in a castle?'

Silently she shook her head.

'Then why don't you try it?' he said persuasively. 'It would be a new experience.'

Through lips that felt oddly stiff, she said, 'No, I'd rather stick to my original plan,' and braced herself to withstand an onslaught.

But, to her surprise, he gave in immediately and with good grace. 'Very well. If that's really what you want…'

Seeing that surprise and knowing he needed to disarm her, he added in a businesslike tone, 'With regard to a hotel, I suggest the Rochester on Crombie Street. It's far from luxurious, but it's pleasant and central and not too expensive.'

'That sounds fine,' she agreed. 'As we'll be late back, it might be as well if I fetch my bag and give them a ring now.'

Damn! he thought. So much for trying to disarm her.

As she started to rise, he pressed her gently back, 'Don't worry, I'll talk to reception while you drink your sherry.'

He crossed to his desk and, picking up the phone, queried, 'Shall I make it tonight *and* tomorrow?'

Already regretting her decision, but knowing it was the right one, she said huskily, 'Please.'

Depressing the receiver rest, he pretended to make the booking.

While she listened, and watched his broad back, she wondered what had made him give in so easily.

The answer came swiftly. Though it would no doubt have suited him if she *had* stayed, it was obviously of no great importance. If *she* wasn't willing, there must be plenty of women who were.

But *she* wasn't cut out for affairs. She couldn't treat sex lightly, or as just another appetite to be indulged, as most men and a lot of today's women seemed able to do.

If Richard had been an ordinary man and she and he had been in love with each other and intending to stay together, it would have been different.

But he wasn't, and they weren't.

And, no matter how much she wanted him, her pride, her self-respect, insisted that she shouldn't let herself be swept up and then discarded at a rich man's whim…

'All settled,' he said, replacing the receiver and returning to his chair by the fire.

'Thank you.' In the end he'd been very civilized about it and she was grateful.

Though she couldn't regret coming to Anders—it would always shine in her memory—she was guiltily aware that, despite his earlier polite denial, he would no doubt regard it as a wasted day.

As though reading her mind, he said, 'I hope you're not sorry you came to the castle?'

'No, I'm not. I've loved being here and seeing over it. The only thing I *am* sorry about is that I've wasted your day.'

'I can assure you I don't regard it as a wasted day. Apart from enjoying your company, which I do very much, it's a pleasure to have someone here who genuinely likes the old place...'

When her sherry was finished, he led the way to a long white-walled dining-room where a refectory table was beautifully set with fine linen, crystal glasses and fresh flowers.

Throughout an excellent meal, as though to put her at her ease, he played the suave host, talking easily about the history of the castle and the Anders family. 'At one time the estate supported a lot of tenant farmers and labourers who owed their allegiance to the family...'

With a little crooked smile that made her heart start to beat faster, he went on, 'It all sounds a bit feudal, doesn't it?'

'It does rather.'

'But, from what I've read in the archives, most of the Anders were good overlords and their serfs and vassals—some of the descendants of whom still live on the estate—were well-treated.'

'How big is the present-day estate?'

He told her, adding, 'It used to be considerably larger. But, before my great-grandfather went into banking, the need to raise money for taxes and death duties had meant selling off certain of the more lucrative areas.

'Luckily there was plenty to go at. The family, who were staunch Royalists, had been given huge tracts of land for their loyalty to the Crown.'

'What happened when Cromwell came to power?'

'It could well have been the end of them all. But when, after the battle of Worcester, a lot of Royalist strongholds were laid waste, because one of Cromwell's closest friends and allies had married Lady Eleanor Anders, the castle and its occupants were mercifully spared…'

As soon as their coffee was finished, Tina—who had been psyching herself up to mention leaving—was about to speak when Richard forestalled her by asking, 'About ready to go?'

'I'll just get my coat and bag.'

'While you do that I'll ring for Mullins to bring your case down and fetch the car round.'

She had just collected her belongings when Richard appeared and said, 'I'm afraid Mullins is out at the moment, but his wife is expecting him back in half an hour or so…'

'Oh,' Tina said a little blankly. 'But can't we—'

'It seems,' Richard added smoothly, 'that he has the car keys in his pocket and unfortunately I've left the spare set in town.'

Before she could think of anything to say, he went on, 'As it's a beautiful moonlit night, I suggest that, rather than just sitting indoors waiting for him, we take a stroll along the battlements.'

Helping her into her coat, he added, 'We may be lucky enough to see our resident ghost.'

Distracted, she exclaimed, 'A ghost?'

'Have you ever seen a ghost?'

She shook her head. 'Have you?'

'No,' he admitted.

'I'm not sure I believe in them.'

'But are you sure you *don't?* There are quite a few sightings of Mag mentioned in the archives.'

'Mag?'

'Today we'd say Maggie, but apparently in the Middle Ages the short form Mag was common.'

Opening the top drawer of a walnut bureau, he took out a pencil torch and slipped it into his pocket. 'Come along then, and I'll tell you all about her as we go.'

Wondering why he needed a torch on a moonlit night, she allowed herself to be escorted to the east tower. There, they climbed the spiralling stone steps and at the top emerged on to the battlements.

The sky was a deep velvety blue with a huge silver disk of moon hanging above the eastern rim of trees. Though it looked shimmering and insubstantial as any mirage, its pale ethereal light was almost as bright as day, yet strangely eerie.

In this kind of setting, she could almost imagine seeing a ghost.

As they started to stroll along the walls, the scented air cool and silky against her face, she shivered a little with nervous excitement.

'Cold?' he asked.

'No, not really.'

He put an arm around her all the same and she found herself glad of it.

'You were going to tell me about your ghost,' she prompted as they walked on.

'According to the legend, Mag was the beautiful and chaste young daughter of Lord Anders's household steward. She fell madly in love with Sir Gerwain, the son of a neighbouring nobleman.

'He told her he loved her and promised that when his elderly father died and he was his own master, he would marry her. They used to meet in Daland Tower, away from prying eyes, and on moonlit nights he would ride over to keep their trysts.

'Mag used to climb up to the battlements to watch for him and when she saw him coming she would slip down a hidden stairway to the cellars and take a secret passage that comes out inside the tower.'

Frowning, Tina asked, 'But what about the moat?'

'The passage runs beneath the moat. It's quite a clever bit of construction.'

With a grin, he added, 'As a boy, it used to be my escape route if I wanted to leave the castle without anyone knowing.'

'Is it still there?'

'Certainly. I could take you through it now if—'

'Oh, yes, please,' she broke in eagerly. It would be another unique memory.

He frowned. 'What about those heels?'

'Is it very rough?'

'A bit tricky in parts, but not a great deal worse than the climb up here.'

'In that case I can manage perfectly well.'

'You don't suffer from claustrophobia?'

'No.'

'Then let's go.' He shepherded her to the west tower, where a low door at the head of the stairway gave on to what appeared to be a short dead-end passage, until his torch showed up a small opening on the left.

'It isn't lit, so I'd better lead the way.'

Stooping a little, the torch lighting up the rough stone, they descended a small stairway hidden in the thickness of the wall until the steps gave way to a low tunnel.

'Go carefully through here,' he warned.

Cramped and narrow, built of old brick with an arched roof, the tunnel sloped downwards for a while before levelling out.

The air was unpleasantly dank, the walls black in parts and slimy to the touch, the hard-packed earth floor decidedly damp and slippery.

Tina was just thinking that she wouldn't be sorry when they

reached the end, when the torch flickered and went out, leaving them in total darkness.

She gave an involuntary gasp and stood quite still. After a second or two she heard a movement and, needing reassurance, reached out to touch him.

But her searching hand found nothing and, in the silence, the terrifying thought popped into her head that he had walked away and abandoned her in this Stygian blackness.

CHAPTER SIX

BITING back the surge of panic, Tina told herself not to be ridiculous and said, 'Richard?' To her everlasting credit, her voice was steady.

'I'm here.' A hand reached out of the pitch-blackness and took hers. 'All right?'

'Yes.'

'I was just checking the torch. I'm afraid the bulb's gone.'

'What do we do now?'

'As we're about halfway, we may as well go on.'

'Very well,' she agreed.

His fingers tightened on hers. 'All you have to do is move slowly and carefully and keep your head down. For a while it's relatively straight and level, then it starts to gradually climb again.'

For what seemed an age, they moved forward at a snail's pace and eventually the ground began to slope upwards. Hampered by her high heels, it became more difficult to keep her footing and her ankle started to throb painfully.

She was accordingly grateful when Richard announced, 'Not far now.'

After a few more yards he released her hand. 'Wait here a moment.'

Once again she experienced that scary feeling of being abandoned in the smothering darkness and was forced to bite her lip.

Then she heard the brush of feet on stone, the scrape of metal on metal and the protesting creak of old hinges. A moment later moonlight came flooding coldly in to illuminate a flight of crumbling steps.

Richard returned to take her hand and they climbed them together, emerging through a small iron-banded door into a roofless half-ruined tower full of bright moonlight and deep shadow.

'So this is where they used to meet,' she said wonderingly.

'Yes. But of course in those days it was merely deserted, not ruined. However, despite the state it's in, it's steeped in history and well worth seeing.'

Closing the door behind them, he turned to look at her and, taking a spotless handkerchief from his pocket, cleaned a smear of black from her cheek. Then, wiping the hand he had used to follow the tunnel wall, he continued, 'However, given the ordeal you've just gone through, you must be sorry you ever agreed to come.'

'No, not at all. It was quite an experience.'

From the picture he'd built up in his mind after reading Grimshaw's reports, he wouldn't have thought her capable of exercising such self-control and the fact that she'd taken things so calmly had both surprised and intrigued him.

Raising her hand to his lips, he said quietly, 'I thought you might go to pieces, but obviously I'd underestimated your courage.'

As he had underestimated her beauty.

Still holding her hand, he looked into her face, made both fascinating and mysterious by the moonlight, his eyes lingering on her mouth.

Flustered by his praise and afraid that if he kissed her she would weaken, she half turned away. 'At least I wasn't alone, as Mag must have been. And presumably she had only a taper or a candle.'

'Which was, I daresay, somewhat more reliable than our torch,' he commented dryly.

Tina had started to smile when, taking her completely by surprise, he turned her into his arms and lifted her face to his. For an instant he looked down at her with queer darkened eyes, then his mouth covered hers.

Her lips parted helplessly beneath the masterful pressure of his and he deepened the kiss, reawakening all the clamouring demons of that morning and sending pleasure coursing through her like red-hot lava.

Lost in a world of sensual delight, she was limp and quivering, almost mindless with desire, when a warning bell began to ring and she stiffened.

His blood heated with anticipation of the night ahead, Richard found it far from easy to play a waiting game, but, feeling that tacit resistance, he ended the kiss and lifted his head.

Drawing a deep, ragged breath, she told herself that she was thankful he'd called a halt. She had virtually no defences against him and if he *hadn't* drawn away when he did, if he'd laid her down there and then on the moonlit grass, she would have been his for the taking.

And he would have thought her easy.

For a moment or two she struggled to pull herself together. When she had, to some extent, succeeded, she found her voice and said a little breathlessly, 'The tower's bigger than I first thought. How many rooms did it have?'

He told her and began to point out where the different floors had once been, where the fireplaces had been situated and where the old stone stairs had spiralled upwards.

When she had seen all there was to see, he turned away and reached to take her hand. Afraid of his touch, afraid of weakening, she pulled it free.

Without comment, he led the way through a gap in the crumbling walls, where long grass and weeds were thrusting up between the fallen stones.

Favouring her bad ankle and trying her best not to hobble, she followed him as best she could.

He made no further attempt to hold her hand; indeed he appeared to be deep in thought as they headed back towards the castle.

They were skirting the beechwood—the glorious blaze of colour bleached to a pale bluey-purple by the moonlight—when, wanting to break the silence, she reminded him, 'You didn't finish telling me what happened to Mag.'

He roused himself and said, 'I'm afraid it's a sad tale. One night, it seems, she waited for Sir Gerwain in vain and the next day she learnt—'

Tina was looking up at him, concentrating on what he was telling her, when her injured ankle turned painfully.

At her little gasp, he stopped speaking abruptly and threw an arm around her to steady her as she wobbled on one leg.

His voice grim, he said, 'I should have had more sense than to take you walking in those heels.'

'I should have had more sense than wear them,' she admitted ruefully.

He took off his jacket and, spreading it on the grass, lowered her on to it. Then, squatting down, he examined her ankle, which was already showing signs of swelling.

'Well, that settles it,' he announced firmly. 'You can't possibly go back to town in this state. The best place for you is bed.'

'Oh, but I—'

Rising to his feet, he said, 'There's no way you can walk on that. A cold compress, a good night's sleep and we'll see how it is in the morning…'

He'd had two objectives and his first had been achieved more or less by chance. Now, with a bit of luck, he could make use of that same chance to achieve his second.

'However,' he went on, 'at the moment our priority is to get you back.'

Gathering herself, she made a valiant attempt to struggle up.

'Stay where you are,' he ordered. 'No doubt we *could* make it back under our own steam, but it's a fair distance, so it would make more sense to have some transport.'

She was waiting for him to say he would walk back and fetch the car, when he asked, 'Do you have your mobile handy? I'm afraid I left mine in my jacket pocket when I changed.'

'Yes.' She fished in her shoulder bag and produced her phone.

'Thanks... I'll ask Mullins to drive round and fetch us...

'Ah, Mullins,' he said after a moment, 'Miss Dunbar has hurt her ankle walking back from Daland Tower. We're by the beechwood, if you could pick us up...'

Then, to Tina, 'He'll be here directly.' Switching off the phone, he slipped it casually into his trousers pocket and sat down beside her, his muscular thigh brushing hers. 'Now, I was telling you about Mag. Where had I got to exactly?'

'One night Sir Gerwain didn't turn up...' she prompted somewhat distractedly.

'Right... Well, the next day, Mag learnt that he was about to marry a lady of rank. A lady he'd been betrothed to since they were both children.

'Left pregnant and alone, Mag threw herself off the battlements into the moat.

'But, if the ghostly legend is to be believed, on moonlit nights she still walks there, waiting for her faithless lover.'

Hearing Tina's sigh, he said, 'I told you it was a sad story.'

'To be honest, I hadn't expected anything else. I've never heard of any ghost who haunted a place because he or she had been happy there.'

His teeth gleamed as he laughed. 'And I always thought it was men who were practical and women who were romantic.'

'Perhaps it is as a rule.'

Looking into her eyes, he said, 'But you're a fascinating mixture of both.' Then, sounding almost surprised, 'I've never met a woman who intrigued me as much as you do.'

The intensity of his gaze was as intimate as a touch. It made her senses reel.

Still gazing into her eyes, he leaned forward and, while she sat there as though mesmerized, touched his lips lightly to hers.

Then, a hand on her nape, he deepened the kiss until there was nothing in the whole world but him and what he was making her feel.

Eyes closed, heart pounding, she had just accepted that she was lost, when he drew away and said, 'Mullins will be here at any moment.'

As he spoke she heard an engine and a second or two later an estate car came bumping over the rough grass towards them.

Richard helped her up and into the car before pulling on his jacket and climbing in beside her.

'If I'm not going back to town tonight—' she spoke the thought aloud '—I ought to let the hotel know.'

'Don't worry,' he said easily. 'I'll take care of that as soon as we get back.'

When they reached the castle, Mullins drove carefully over the cobbled courtyard and, stopping by the impressive door, got out to open it, while Richard came round to Tina's side and, stooping, instructed, 'Put your arms round my neck.'

When she obeyed, he lifted her out effortlessly and carried her inside, saying to Mullins on the way, 'Thanks and goodnight.'

'Goodnight, sir, madam.'

'Goodnight,' Tina said huskily.

Though she tried to stay calm, being held in Richard's arms and cradled against his broad chest made her heart start to throw itself against her ribcage and her breathing quicken and grow ragged.

Since she had first seen him standing in Cartel's loading

bay she had been drawn to him, fascinated by him, beguiled and bewitched.

And that dark enchantment and the sexual tension that accompanied it had never slackened. In fact it had increased, so that she no longer trusted her ability to be strong, to follow the course she had set herself...

But somehow she had to hide that growing weakness, otherwise he would take advantage of it and then she would lose what little was left of her pride...

As he carried her up the stairs and into his suite she realised that, like the previous night, though *her* breathing had quickened, his hadn't altered in the slightest.

Carrying her through to the guest room, he said, 'I presume, from all you said earlier, that you'd prefer to sleep here.'

It was a statement rather than a question and it made it easier to answer, 'Yes, thank you. I would,' and sound as if she meant it.

When she had dropped her bag on the nearest chair he carried her into the bathroom and, setting her down carefully, helped her off with her coat before asking, 'Shall I ring for one of the maids?'

'Oh, no. There's no need to disturb anyone so late. I can manage perfectly well.'

'In that case I'll fetch your bag.'

Returning with them almost immediately, he queried, 'Sure you're all right for the moment?'

'Quite sure, thank you.'

'Then I'll ring the hotel and find some strapping for that ankle.'

Handicapped as she was, it took her longer than usual to shower, clean her teeth and put on her nightdress and gown. Finally, warm and dry and scented, she brushed out her long corn-gold hair. Normally, for bed, she braided it, but, fearing a plait might look childish, she returned to the bedroom with it loose around her shoulders.

He was sitting in one of the low chairs, his long legs stretched out, his ankles crossed negligently.

Rising to his feet at her approach, he said lightly, 'All ready with the first aid kit.'

'I'm sorry to have been so long,' she apologized.

'Considering the difficulties, I think you've been re-markably quick…'

He turned the quilt back. 'Now, then, if you'd like to get into bed, I'll take a look at that ankle.'

Her calf-length nightdress was relatively modest and, slipping off her gown, she got into bed, praying he would do what he needed to do and go quickly.

When she was settled against the pillows, he examined her ankle once more, his strong fingers gently probing the slight swelling.

Seeing her wince, he said, 'It should be a lot less painful once it's strapped up.'

Taking a pad soaked in something cold and a stretch bandage, he sat down on the edge of the bed and proceeded to deftly apply them.

'There—' he tucked the end in neatly '—how does that feel?'

'Much better already, thank you.'

'With a bit of luck it will be as good as new by morning.' He rose to his feet and pulled the quilt up in preparation for going.

She was just breathing a sigh of relief when he sat down again and studied her face. 'You look a bit pale and tense; would you like a hot drink and a couple of painkillers before I leave you?'

Very conscious of him, she shook her head. 'Thank you, but I don't really need them. My ankle's fine while I'm lying down. It only hurts when I try to put any weight on it…' Realising that nervousness was making her babble, she stopped abruptly.

'Then if there's nothing else I can do for you, I'll say goodnight.'

Leaning over, he kissed her, his mouth brushing hers lightly, seductively. Then, his lips tracing the soft underside of her chin and travelling down the creamy column of her throat, he whispered, 'Unless you've changed your mind about sharing my bed?'

Feeling as though she was drowning in honey, she struggled against the temptation to say she had. Though she couldn't remember anything about it, she was no longer a virgin, so what had she got to lose?

Her self-respect, that was what! And it was important to her. Last night she had been drunk and unable to help herself, but tonight she was stone cold sober and responsible for her actions.

'I want to make love to you,' he murmured softly, while his hands found the soft curves of her breasts and the firming nipples beneath the thin satin of her nightdress, 'I want to sleep with you in my arms, to wake to find you beside me and make love to you all over again… Tell me you want it, too…'

Her lips moved, but no sound came.

'Tell me,' he insisted.

'I can't!' It was almost a sob. 'I can't…'

'Why can't you? I know you want me. Your whole body's telling me so.'

'I've never…' She swallowed hard, then went on desperately, 'I've never gone in for one-night stands or casual sex and I don't want to start now.'

He frowned a little. 'Who said anything about a one-night stand or casual sex? Neither the way I feel about you, nor my intentions are in any way casual.'

His words held a ring of truth and her heart leapt. If it really *was* true, it altered everything.

Then common sense told her not to be foolish. How could he feel anything for her when they'd only known each other for twenty-four hours?

But why couldn't he?

What she felt for him, whether she called it infatuation or falling in love, was anything but casual. In fact it was so strong, so overwhelming, it made anything she had felt for Kevin fade into insignificance.

Shaken and confused, she stared down at the old patchwork quilt, its colours faded and mellowed by time, while a part of her mind, standing detached, aloof, thought how pretty it was.

After a moment or two when, head bent, she remained silent, he rose to his feet and said evenly, 'Sleep well. I'll see you in the morning.'

She watched him head for the door, her thoughts racing. Just for the sake of her pride or the fear of what the future might hold, was she going to let him walk away? Turn her back on this chance to be with him? If it all ended in tears, at least she would have known some happiness...

His hand was on the latch when she spoke his name.

Though her voice was barely above a whisper, he turned and looked at her.

'Please don't go.'

He came to the side of the bed and, his handsome face alight with satisfaction and triumph, asked, 'You've never slept in a centuries-old four-poster on a goosefeather bed?'

'No.' Nor did she know what it was like to sleep in a man's arms.

Pulling back the quilt, he scooped her up. 'Then this will be a first.'

In the master bedroom, which was unlit save for a log fire that blazed cheerfully in the wide stone hearth, the air smelt pleasantly of pine-resin, beeswax and lavender. The pillows on the splendid four-poster had been plumped up and the bedclothes turned down invitingly.

He carried her over to the bed, which was so high that on either side there was a wooden step up to it, and laid her down. Saying, 'We won't need this,' he eased her nightdress over her head and tossed it aside, before pulling up the covers.

When he had quickly stripped off his own clothes and hung them over a chair, he disappeared into the bathroom, promising softly, 'I won't be long.'

As the door closed behind him, some lines from an anonymous poem began to run through her head:

> The day had faded fast and gone,
> and in that shining night,
> he offered me a precious gift,
> a promise of delight…

A thrill of excitement and anticipation ran through her, making her breath catch in her throat and her heart beat erratically.

Moonlight gleamed on the casements and somewhere close at hand an owl hooted with melancholy mirth, while in the grate a log slipped and settled, sending up a shower of bright sparks and making long shadows dance across the ceiling.

The bathroom door opened and he came out, his dark hair still damp from the shower and without a stitch on, as she had seen him that morning.

Was it only that morning? It seemed so long ago.

She had thought then what a magnificent male animal he was. Now, she couldn't take her eyes off him. Every bone in her body seemed to melt with longing and her entire being cried out for his possession.

Her face must have registered what she was thinking and feeling, because he said in a voice shaken between passion and laughter, 'When you look at me like that you make me feel like Suleiman.'

He slid beneath the covers and joined her.

The moment he touched her she began to tremble.

Running his hands down her slender body and feeling her response, he said softly, 'You're all fizz and sparkle, like champagne.

'But though champagne is heady and exhilarating, it's light, surface stuff.'

Taking first one pink nipple in his mouth and then the other, he suckled sweetly while his long fingers found the silken warmth of her inner thighs.

Not wanting it to be over almost before it had begun, she tried to push his hand away, to hold back. But he would have none of it.

A few seconds later she gave a little cry as sensation followed sensation, like surface ripples on a pool that spread in ever-widening circles round a flung stone.

When the sensations had died away, unconsciously she sighed. Though he had given her a great deal of pleasure, she had wanted the experience to be a *shared* one...

As she lay with closed eyes, he kissed her and said, 'Now the fizz has been disposed of we can go on to enjoy something altogether deeper and more rewarding, like a rich, satisfying Burgundy.'

His hands began to move lightly over her, stroking and caressing, making each nerve-ending spring into life and effortlessly reviving the desire she had thought sated.

By the time he fitted himself into the cradle of her hips, eager for his possession, she welcomed his weight. Even so, his first strong thrust made her gasp and, as though taken by surprise, he paused and asked, 'Did I hurt you?'

'Yes... No... It doesn't matter.' With an instinct as old as Eve, she lifted her hips enticingly and he began to move again, but a little more cautiously.

'All right?' he queried after a moment or two.

Caught up now in a spiralling pleasure, she was past answering, but her flung back head and soft gasping cries were answer enough.

Reassured, he carried them both to a shattering climax that sent them tumbling and spinning through time and space.

Wrapped in black velvet, the sensations so deep and intense that she was shaken to the very core of her being, she lay beneath him, shuddering helplessly.

At the same time she felt exalted, omnipotent, the feel of his flesh against hers and the weight of his dark head on her breast a priceless gift.

She knew a sudden poignant happiness. He was her man. Her mate. Her *love*.

So this was what love was really like, what all the love songs and poetry added up to. Two people coming together and meeting on every level, a meeting as much spiritual as physical.

She could only feel glad that, instead of giving herself lightly for a moment's gratification, she had waited for this one man.

When their breathing and heart rate returned to something like normal, he lifted himself away and turned on his back. Then, gathering her close, he settled her head comfortably at the juncture between chest and shoulder and, his arm holding her securely, bent his head to kiss her.

His kiss seemed gentle and caring and she found herself hoping against hope that he shared at least some of her feelings.

After a little while she became aware of a quiet but persistent thought tugging at the sleeve of her consciousness, trying to gain her attention. Still euphoric, unwilling to think, she mentally waved it away. But refusing to be banished, it became even more insistent.

It was another moment or two before she identified it, then surprise made her blurt out what she was now certain of. 'You *didn't* make love to me… Last night, I mean…'

'No,' he agreed.

'But I thought… Though I couldn't remember, I was sure we'd slept together…'

'So we had. That is to say, we slept in the same bed. That's all.'

'I don't understand why…'

She felt the movement as he glanced down at her. 'You went

out like a light so, apart from taking off your clothes, I never laid a finger on you. I cursed myself for getting you in that state, but by then it was too late.'

'But you said we'd…'

Realising he'd never actually *said* anything, she changed it to, 'You deliberately made me think we'd slept together.'

'When you jumped to that conclusion, I just didn't correct you.'

And she could guess why not. With her believing they were already lovers, tonight's seduction had been so much easier. Had she known the truth, would she have behaved differently?

But it was too late to ask herself that.

'Mad with me?' he queried.

She ought to be.

But she wasn't really.

How could she be mad with a man who had given her so much, and with such tenderness?

'No,' she whispered.

His arm tightened round her.

Beneath her cheek she could feel the strong, steady beat of his heart, hear the quiet evenness of his breathing, smell the scent of his skin, with its heady combination of fresh perspiration and shower gel.

It was so sweet, so intimate, that she gave thanks as she lay blissfully savouring the warmth and happiness, the feeling of belonging, of having finally come home.

She was still marvelling at the peace and beauty of it when sleep crept up and wrapped her in a soft, dark blanket.

Next morning she awoke to full remembrance and a singing happiness. A smile on her lips, she turned her head to look at Richard, but she was alone in the big four-poster.

Sunshine was streaming in through the leaded glass of the

windows and a glance at her watch showed it was almost a quarter to nine.

Some time during the night he had wakened her with a kiss and made long, delectable love to her once more and, though a little tender in parts, her body felt as sleek and well-satisfied as a pampered pedigree cat.

She stretched luxuriously, while her mind drifted on a cloud of euphoria. She had found her one and only love. He filled her heart and banished her loneliness, satisfied a gnawing hunger that had never been fed.

He was so right for her. He had strength and humour, warmth and understanding, a willingness to reach out, to meet her on her own ground.

Yet, like herself, he had a certain reserve, so there would always be thoughts and dreams to surprise. An element of spice to keep their relationship fresh.

Their relationship…

Like a train hitting the buffers, her rhapsodizing came to an abrupt halt. Could she call what they had a *relationship*?

Why not? she thought boldly. Though it was still in its early stages, it *was* a relationship. Hadn't he made it clear that his feelings and his intentions weren't merely casual?

It was a start and if, in spite of their vastly different backgrounds and lifestyles, he could come to care for her, she could ask no more of life.

And if he couldn't?

She pushed the intrusive thought away.

At least she knew what it was like to really be in love, and it was a marvellous feeling! No wonder people said that love made the world go round.

All at once she wanted to say it out loud, to shout it from the rooftops.

Bubbling over with excitement, she decided that as soon as she had showered and dressed she would ring her flatmate.

Normally, she wouldn't have made contact until Jules had gone back to Paris, but her news was so exciting she just couldn't wait to tell somebody.

Ruth, who knew nothing of the weekend's events and still thought Tina was staying in London with one of their friends, would be surprised, to say the least. But when she had heard everything, she would understand and be pleased...

Climbing out of the high bed, Tina cautiously tested her ankle. Finding it supported her without pain, she gathered up her discarded nightdress and, her bare feet squeaking a little on the polished oak floorboards, made her way back to the guest room.

Fresh and glowing from the shower, she brushed her blonde hair and, leaving it loose around her shoulders, pulled on clean underwear, a pair of cream trousers and a silky shirt the colour of burnt toffee.

Her ankle had returned to virtually normal, so she left the strapping off and donned flat slip-ons, all the time anticipating Ruth's reaction to her wonderful news.

She had located her bag and started to fish around for her phone before she recalled that Richard had borrowed it the previous evening and must have absent-mindedly pocketed it.

Well, she would have to find him and ask him for it. Unless... On an impulse she returned to the master bedroom, where the suit he had worn had been hung over a chair. Locating his jacket, after a momentary hesitation, she felt in the nearest pocket.

There was no sign of her phone, but her fingers closed around his pencil torch which lit as she inadvertently pressed the button.

So the bulb hadn't gone after all. If Richard had paused long enough to double-check, it would have saved that long, slow, nightmare journey through the Stygian passageway.

The second pocket yielded nothing more than the handkerchief he had wiped her cheek with, and only then did she recall that she had been *sitting* on his jacket. Which meant he must have slipped the phone into his trousers pocket.

Feeling uncomfortable, but *committed* now, she gritted her teeth and searched both pockets, but once again she drew a blank.

Oh, well, she would just have to go down and ask him what he'd done with it.

Her step light, a smile on her lips as she imagined how he'd lift her face to his and kiss her, she left the suite and descended the elegant oak staircase.

As she paused to stroke the lion's head on the newel post, Hannah appeared in the hall, neat and Sundayish in a sober black hat, a prayer book in her gloved hand.

'Good morning, Miss Dunbar. I hope you slept well?'

Feeling her cheeks grow warm at the innocent enquiry, Tina answered, 'Very well, thank you, Hannah. You're off to church?'

Her manner prim, Hannah said, 'It's customary for all the staff to attend the Sunday morning service at our own chapel.'

Flustered by her previous lack of thought, Tina hastened to say, 'Of course. It must be a great blessing to have a resident priest.'

'Indeed it is,' Hannah told her. Adding proudly, 'The Reverend Peter has been in the family's service and lived in the rooms adjoining the chapel ever since he was ordained nearly fifty years ago.'

'What a wonderful record.'

'Apart from the mistress's second marriage, which took place in a register office, he's officiated at every wedding, christening and funeral of both the family and the staff.

'It's his dearest wish, before he's called to his maker, to officiate at the master's wedding.

'When Miss O'Connell's family first moved into Farrington Hall and the young couple became friendly, we began to wonder if she might be the one. But after the mistress's death, Mr Richard no longer came home and Miss O'Connell stopped calling…'

Beaming, as if Tina should be pleased too, she went on, 'But now—though Mr Richard has made it clear that it's still unofficial—we're delighted by the news that at long last the Reverend Peter is going to have his wish…'

So Richard was going to be married.

'Well, I must get along. The master was in the study earlier, if you're looking for him…' Her back ramrod straight, Hannah hurried away.

CHAPTER SEVEN

COLD and sick and shattered, Tina stood stricken, unable to move, knowing how Mag must have felt.

In her ears was his voice saying, 'Who said anything about a one-night stand or casual sex? Neither the way I feel about you, nor my intentions are in any way casual'… And, fool that she was, she had believed his lies.

Unless he was planning on having an ongoing affair *after* he was married?

Well, if he was, she thought bitterly, he could count her out.

When she had recovered enough to move, her first impulse was to run and hide. To leave his home and never see him again. But she had no way of leaving unless she could find a phone and call for a taxi.

There must be phones at the castle but, apart from the one in the library-cum-study that Richard had used the previous night, she hadn't noticed any. Perhaps, like the television, they were hidden away.

But all that was beside the point; she needed her own mobile. So somehow she had to face him, to tell him she was leaving. But if she wanted to go with some shred of pride intact, she had, somehow, to hide just how shattered she felt.

On legs that trembled so much they would scarcely carry her, she made her way across the hall to the study. As she was passing the living-room door, which was a little ajar, she heard Richard's voice and, pausing, once again found herself eavesdropping on a phone conversation.

'As the time factor is of overriding importance,' he was saying, 'there isn't a moment to lose—'

Only it *wasn't* a phone conversation, she realised a second later, as a woman's voice broke in, 'But surely it's already too late. It just can't be done in the time.'

'It *can* be done,' Richard insisted quietly. 'In fact the arrangements are already in place.'

Feeling like death, lacking the will to walk away, Tina listened dully to the argument.

'There must be some other way,' the woman insisted shrilly. 'You're not short of money; couldn't you—?'

'That was my first thought, but money isn't necessarily the answer. I don't know for sure what I'm up against, and by the time I *do* know it'll be too late.'

'But Richard—' It was a wail.

'It's no use, Helen, I simply can't afford to chance doing it any other way…'

Helen… Helen O'Connell. So it was his future wife he was talking to.

'It's only too easy to be held to ransom and drained dry. But once I'm in a position of strength, my money can be used to greater effect.'

'But it's so…so *drastic.*'

'I've given it a lot of thought and I'm satisfied that it's by far the safest option.'

'What do you suppose will happen when—?'

'There's bound to be a backlash of course,' he broke in a trifle curtly, 'but I'll deal with that as and when it happens.'

'Well, I think you're making a dreadful mistake.' Then, with a flare of hope, 'You could always fight it through the courts.'

'I considered that, of course, but it might take years and, as things stand at present, there's no guarantee I'd win.'

'But have you considered the ethics of it?'

'You mean two wrongs don't make a right?' he suggested a shade grimly. 'Oh, yes, I've considered all that. But I'll do whatever it takes. As far as I'm concerned, the end justifies the means. I've far too much to lose to think of playing Sir Galahad…'

Standing, shivering and miserable, outside the living-room door, Tina was chilled anew by the icy ruthlessness in his voice.

This was a side of him that she hadn't yet seen. But perhaps, as a successful businessman, he needed to have a ruthless streak.

Though his future wife didn't seem to care for it. Sounding close to breaking-point, she cried, 'Well, I still think you're wrong. There has to be a better way…' Then, with a touch of venom, 'Unless, of course, it's really what you want…'

As she heard the doorknob rattle beneath fumbling fingers, terrified of being caught eavesdropping, Tina turned to run.

Knowing she would never make it across the hall and up the stairs without being seen, she fled into the neighbouring study just as the living-room door opened and closed.

Through the window, which overlooked the courtyard, she could see a bright red open-topped sports car standing by the main entrance, sun ricocheting from its polished bonnet.

A few seconds later the front door opened and a tall, slim, dark-haired woman came hurrying out with Richard at her heels.

While he had remained calm and implacable, the argument—whatever it had been about—had clearly upset Helen O'Connell and she was in tears.

His face showing concern now, he made an obvious attempt to reason with her.

When, beside herself, she refused to listen, he took her arm. She pulled it free. He tried again to detain her but, with sudden unbridled fury, she turned and slapped his face.

Then, jumping into the car, she started the ignition,

stamped her foot down and, with a reckless burst of acceleration, roared across the cobbles, through the archway and over the bridge.

Richard stood for a moment, his hand to his cheek, staring after her.

When he turned to make his way back inside, afraid that he might see her watching, Tina hurriedly moved away from the window.

She was heading for the door when, unwilling to chance running into him in the hall in case he guessed what she had seen and heard, she hesitated. It might be safest to stay where she was until the coast was clear.

The next second found her wondering if that was the right decision. He'd obviously been working in here when his visitor had arrived and a file had been tossed down and left on his desk.

Suppose he came straight back to the study?

Knowing she was trapped, she waited in an agony of suspense, listening for his approaching footsteps, wondering how best to explain her presence there.

When several minutes had dragged past without her hearing a sound, realising that he *wasn't* coming straight back, she heaved a sigh of relief.

If she used the phone on the desk to ring for a taxi and arranged to meet it at the top of the drive rather than let it come through into the courtyard, she might be able to leave without anyone knowing.

It would mean going without her mobile, but that was a small price to pay.

She was just reaching for the receiver when, without warning, the door opened, making her gasp.

A second later Richard walked in, looking coolly elegant in well-cut fawn trousers and a short-sleeved olive-green silk shirt open at the neck.

'So there you are,' he said, his taut expression clearing.

'When you weren't upstairs I started to wonder where you'd got to. How's the ankle this morning? It looks as if the swelling's gone down…'

Appearing relaxed and easy now, he came over and, tilting her chin, kissed her mouth.

A lover's kiss.

For a split second she stood as though turned to stone, then, on a reflex action, she jerked her head sharply away.

His dark level brows drawing together in a frown, he queried, 'What's the matter?'

Momentarily unable to speak, she shook her head.

'Something must be.'

'I couldn't find my phone,' she said in a rush, 'and I wanted to call a taxi.'

'Why do you want a taxi?' he asked evenly.

'Because I'm leaving.'

His tawny eyes narrowed. 'What's happened to make you want to leave?'

'Nothing,' she lied desperately. 'I just think it's time I went. So, if you don't mind—'

'Oh, but I do.' Suddenly he was looming over her. 'After all we've shared, I mind very much that you want to walk out without any explanation.'

Gritting her teeth, she said boldly, 'I don't have to give an explanation. Surely the fact that I want to leave is enough. Now, if you'll please let me have my mobile back.'

When he merely looked at her, she reminded him, 'You kept it last night after you'd called Mullins—'

'In that case it must be in my pocket…'

Shaking her head, she began, 'It isn't—'

He raised a dark brow. 'How do you know?'

Seeing her flush guiltily, he observed, 'So you've been going through my pockets?'

'I'm sorry,' she said jerkily. 'I should have asked you, I

know, but I'm afraid I acted on impulse…' The explanation petered out.

'And did you find anything interesting?' he queried with smooth mockery.

Nettled by his tone, she flashed back, 'Only a torch that lit.'

'Really?' he drawled. 'Then there must have been a loose connection.'

When he said nothing further, deciding to let it go, she gritted her teeth and returned to the point. 'So please can I have my mobile?'

'If it isn't in my pocket, I'm afraid…' With an elegant gesture of apology, he spread his hands, palms upward.

'I don't believe you don't know where it is.'

'And I don't believe that you suddenly want to leave Anders for no good reason.'

Realising that she was fighting a losing battle, she said shortly, 'Whatever you believe, you can't prevent me from going.'

'Don't be too sure about that.'

Suddenly scared, she brushed past him, catching the edge of the file that was lying on his desk, knocking it to the floor and spreading the contents.

Even as she stepped over the papers and headed for the door, part of her mind registered the fact that several of them bore a stylized logo.

Her hand was on the knob when Richard caught her arm and swung her round. Then, turning the big key in the lock, he dropped it into his trousers pocket and stooped to gather together the contents of the file.

As he dropped it back on his desk, she faced him defiantly. 'You can't keep me here against my will.'

'Maybe not for any length of time,' he admitted. 'But certainly for the moment.'

'I insist that you let me go.'

'Even if I did, it would be extremely difficult for you to

leave without some kind of transport… So suppose you tell me the truth.'

Biting her lip, she said nothing.

'I can only presume it's something to do with Helen's visit,' he hazarded. 'Something you overheard, perhaps?'

When she remained stubbornly silent, he sighed.

'What a shame the thumbscrews aren't handy,' she taunted with sudden recklessness.

Between thick dark lashes his eyes gleamed green as a cat's. 'There are other ways.'

Though he spoke lightly, she felt her blood run cold. Still she braved it out. 'Such as?'

He smiled mirthlessly. 'Judging by the way you shied away when I kissed you, I gather you'd prefer me not to touch you?'

She lifted her chin defiantly. 'You're quite right, I would.'

'You didn't seem to feel that way last night.'

'I do now.'

A little smile playing around his chiselled mouth, with slow deliberation he began to unbutton his shirt before pulling it from the waistband of his trousers.

'What are you doing?' she cried, aghast.

'Taking off my clothes. Perhaps you'd like to do the same?'

'No, I wouldn't.'

'Well, I could take them off for you,' he suggested. 'On the other hand, I haven't made love fully clothed since I was an impetuous teenager, so it might be something of a novelty.'

'I don't want you to make love to me,' she cried in a strangled voice. 'I don't want you to touch me.'

'So you said. But if you really don't want that, then you'll tell me why you're so intent on leaving.' When she stayed mute, with a suddenness that took her completely by surprise, he pulled her close and, neatly hooking her feet from beneath her, followed her down, his arms breaking her fall.

Flat on her back on the thick-pile carpet, she made an

attempt to struggle free but, catching her wrists, he pinned them over her head.

His shirt was open and, looking up at his broad chest, the strong column of his neck, the tender hollow at the base, she felt her stomach clench.

As calmly as possible, she said, 'Let me go.'

By way of answer, he put his lips to the pulse fluttering wildly in her throat.

Thickly, she insisted, 'If you don't let me go this instant I'll scream.'

His smile maddeningly cool, he said, 'Do you think I'd allow you to? In any case, there's no one to hear you. All the household servants are at chapel.'

He brought her wrists together and, holding them in one hand, used the other to unfasten the buttons of her blouse.

Then, flicking it open, he ran a fingertip beneath the edge of her low-cut bra and heard her breathing quicken even more. His finger delved a little deeper and he watched with satisfaction as her nipples firmed visibly beneath the delicate material.

Still she held out and he bent his head.

Feeling the heat and dampness of his mouth through the satin and lace, she began to shudder. 'Don't,' she whispered in desperation. 'Don't…'

'Why not? You liked it last night.'

'That was before…'

'Before what?'

She threw in the towel. 'Before I knew you were planning to get married.'

'Ah,' he said softly, 'so that's it.' Then, quick as a rattlesnake striking, 'How do you know I'm planning to get married?'

'Hannah mentioned it.'

He relaxed a little. 'When did you see Hannah?'

'I met her as I was coming downstairs. She was on her way to the chapel.'

'I see. So that's what all the fuss is about.'

'If you're going to try and tell me it isn't true—'

'I've no intention of telling you any such thing.'

'Oh…' Perhaps even now she had been treasuring some faint hope that Hannah had got it wrong.

Irony in his voice, he asked, 'As you know I'm getting married, perhaps you also know who my bride-to-be is?'

'Yes, I do. It's Helen O'Connell.'

He raised a dark brow. 'What makes you presume that? It's not just because she came here, surely?'

'It's what I understood from Hannah.'

Frowning, he suggested, 'Perhaps you'd better tell me word for word exactly what Hannah said.'

As near as she could remember, Tina repeated what the housekeeper had told her, adding with unconscious bitterness, 'I gather she's delighted.'

'But you're not?'

'As far as I'm concerned, Miss O'Connell is more than welcome to you.'

'Jealous?'

'No, I'm not.'

'Tell me,' he said, his face sardonic, 'if you're not jealous, why are you so angry about it?'

Made furious by his cavalier attitude, she cried, 'Because you're a brute and a beast and an unfeeling devil! How *could* you bring me here like this? What would your fiancée think if she found out?'

'Do I take it you're planning to tell her?' he asked mockingly.

'No, I'm not. The only thing I'm planning is to go and never get within a mile of you again.'

He shook his head regretfully. 'In that case I'm afraid our schedules don't match. You see I have no intention of letting you go and every intention of keeping you close by my side.'

Bending his head, he kissed her.

The casual arrogance of that kiss was the last straw and she began to struggle furiously, writhing and kicking, fighting to free her hands.

She was young and fit and, despite her slender build, strong.

But he was so much stronger.

Holding her down with the weight of his body, he ordered, 'Lie still or you'll hurt yourself.'

When, from sheer exhaustion, she was forced to obey, he said quietly, 'That's better.'

'Oh, please, Richard,' she begged raggedly, 'let me get up.'

Perhaps he realised how close to tears she was, because without further ado he released her wrists and his weight lifted from her.

Having helped her up, he rebuttoned her blouse before pushing her gently into the nearest chair. Then, having fastened his own shirt and tucked it into the waistband of his trousers, he stood looking down at her.

All trace of mockery gone now, he said, 'I want you to listen to me. You're right in thinking that I'm hoping to be married…'

Fool that she was, she had still half hoped that he might deny it.

'However, you're quite wrong in believing that the lady in question is Helen O'Connell…'

'Oh…' Tina said in a small voice.

'At one time Hannah may have had hopes in that direction but, when she mentioned the Reverend Peter getting his wish, you were mistaken in thinking she was referring to Helen.'

Feeling foolish, Tina stared blindly down at her hands clasped together in her lap.

When she said nothing, he went on evenly, 'Because Hannah's been part of the family for so long, I told her my plans… Though I must admit I hadn't expected her to say anything until I'd had a chance to discuss those plans with the woman I'm hoping to marry.'

When Tina continued to sit in silence, head bent, the mockery back in his voice, he suggested, 'Now aren't you going to ask me who that woman is?'

She shook her head. It didn't really matter who it was. The mere fact that he had found a woman he wanted to marry had turned her own short-lived happiness into dust and ashes.

'Does that mean you're not interested, or you feel reluctant to ask?'

Apart from saying that his intentions were in no way casual, he'd made no commitment, had promised her nothing, so what right had she to ask?

'Well?' he pressed.

'I feel I've no right to ask,' she admitted dully.

A hand beneath her chin, he lifted her face and said firmly, 'After the way I've treated you, you've *every* right to ask.'

Her breath taken away, she gazed up at him mutely as he went on, 'I got you to come here by offering you a job. A job you turned down on the grounds that, because we'd been to bed together, you would find it awkward to work for me.

'That shows a rare sensitivity in this day and age, when a lot of women wouldn't have given it a second thought or would have regarded a sexual interest as a plus.

'Well, now I'm offering you a different kind of job, a job where a sexual interest is not only a plus but absolutely vital…'

When, her blue-violet eyes wide, she continued to stare up at him, he said, 'I want *you* to be my wife.'

'What?' she whispered, unable to believe her ears.

'I want *you* to be my wife,' he repeated. 'Or, as Marlowe put it, "Come live with me and be my love…"'

'It's sudden, I admit,' he added quizzically, 'but there's no need to look quite so taken aback. After all, I did make it plain that my interest was far from casual…'

'Yes, I know, but I… I never thought… I never dreamt…' Wanting to believe it, but afraid to, needing desperately to be reassured that this wasn't some kind of cruel joke, she asked huskily, 'Do you really want to marry me?'

'Yes,' he answered, a touch of amusement in his voice, 'I really do.'

When, still struggling to take it in, she said nothing, he offered teasingly, 'Would you like me to say it again?'

'I—I'm sorry, but I just find it hard to believe,' she admitted.

'But my proposal isn't unwelcome, I hope?' A finger tracing the curve of her cheek, he asked with apparent irrelevance, 'When we saw the evening star and both made a wish, what did you wish for?'

Seeing her colour rise, he smiled, as if that was answer enough, and told her softly, '*You* are what *I* wished for.' Bending his head, he kissed her lips. A light coaxing kiss. 'All you have to do is marry me to make my wish come true.

'I would have waited a little and proposed to you in a more romantic setting,' he added seriously, 'if Hannah hadn't let the cat out of the bag.

'However,' he went on after a moment, 'I hope the setting won't make any difference to your answer?'

The setting wasn't important, Tina thought, winging her way up to cloud nine—Richard loved her and wanted to marry her; that was all that mattered.

She would have been content with his love—more than content, deliriously happy. The fact that he wanted to make her his wife was more than she had ever dared to hope for and her heart swelled with joy and gratitude.

Watching her glowing face, he was almost sure that he'd pulled it off. But he needed to hear her say it out loud.

When she continued to sit as though in a trance, her eyes soft and full of dreams, growing impatient, he took her shoulders and, lifting her to her feet, urged, 'I'm still waiting for an answer. Will you marry me?'

She gave him the most glorious smile and answered simply, 'Yes.'

That smile made him feel despicable and, for a split second, in spite of everything, he wondered if he was doing the right thing.

But he couldn't afford to weaken now.

Shrugging off the feeling, he hardened his heart.

Though it was over in an instant, she picked up that fleeting doubt. 'But perhaps we should have time to think it over?'

He frowned. 'Do you need time?'

She shook her head. 'No, not really. But I thought *you* might.'

'*I* don't need time to think it over. I know exactly what I'm doing.'

'But you don't really know enough about me.'

'I know everything I need to know.'

Though he sounded certain, a lingering unease made her ask, 'On the drive here you talked about your wife and children living at Anders… Suppose I dislike children and don't want any…?'

'*Do* you dislike children?'

'No, of course I don't. I don't think a marriage is complete without children, but—'

His mouth covered hers, stopping the words, before he said, 'Then I know everything I need to know.'

'How can you be so sure when we only met a couple of days ago?'

'The first time I saw you I knew you were all I'd ever dreamed of or wanted in a woman.'

Though his answer was sweet and romantic, something impelled her to say, 'It just seems so sudden…'

He brushed her lips lightly with his. 'Have you never heard of love at first sight?'

'Of course, but—'

'I had hoped the feeling might have been mutual.'

After a moment she admitted softly, 'It was.'

Making no attempt to hide his elation, he pulled her into his arms and began to kiss her in earnest.

For a while they stood embracing, lost to the world, like Donne's ecstatic lovers.

Eventually, the intrusive thought that there were still things to be done, one final hurdle to surmount, disturbed the blissful mood.

Lifting his head reluctantly and opting for a change of scene, Richard suggested, 'It's a lovely morning—shall we get some fresh air?'

A fountain of happiness welling inside her, she nodded. 'Let's.'

'Sure the ankle's up to it?'

'It's as good as new this morning.'

'Oh, wait a minute, you won't have had anything to eat yet…'

'I haven't, but—'

'There'll be bacon and eggs and coffee keeping hot in the breakfast room.'

'I'm not hungry, but I'd like a cup of coffee before we go.'

When they'd each had a coffee, wondering how best to play it without appearing to rush things, he suggested casually, 'Would you like to stroll down and see the horses?'

'I'd love to.'

'You said you used to ride.'

'Oh, yes. Though I haven't been on a horse for some time now, I rode a lot when I was younger.'

'Then perhaps we could take them out.'

He captured her hand and laced his fingers through hers as they left the breakfast room and made their way along the length of the hall.

Beyond the servants' quarters, the kitchens and a flagged outer hall—all of which appeared to be deserted—a huge studded-oak door opened on to a wide area of decking and a sturdy wooden bridge.

'The tradesmen's entrance,' Richard told her with a grin as they crossed the bridge hand in hand.

It was a beautiful morning, calm and sunny, the balmy air full of the oddly poignant scents of autumn: freshly sawn pine logs, late wallflowers, decaying leaves and woodsmoke.

On the far side of the bridge was a paved carriageway, one fork of which served the garden area, while the other, running between smooth lawns, sloped gently down to an old-fashioned stone-built stable block and coach house.

The large central archway was surmounted by a cupola, on top of which a black wrought iron weathervane—a horse taking the place of the traditional cock—stood motionless in the still air.

On all four sides of the cupola was a large clock with a blue face and golden hands that declared it was almost ten-thirty.

In the stable yard a short bow-legged man wearing a flat cap, a flannel shirt and riding breeches was grooming a large black stallion, whose coat gleamed with good health and care.

'Morning, Josh,' Richard said cheerfully. 'I'd like you to meet Miss Dunbar.'

'Good morning, miss… Morning, Mr Richard.' The groom touched his forelock in a gesture Tina had thought obsolete.

Indicating a chestnut mare with pricked ears and gentle eyes who was regarding them quietly over one of the stable doors, Richard told her, 'This is Juno.'

'Well, hello…' Tina stroked the waiting head and was nuzzled in return. 'You're beautiful…'

'And, as you've no doubt guessed, this is Jupiter.' Richard clapped the black horse on the shoulder.

Taking a liking to the big placid-looking animal, she stroked his velvety muzzle and told him, 'My, but you're a handsome fellow…'

Lifting his head, he snuffled her cheek appreciatively.

'If you were thinking of taking un out,' Josh said, 'I can have un saddled up in no time at all.'

'What about Juno?' Richard asked.

'Yesterday when 'er was out, 'er cast a near hind shoe. I'm

waiting on Tom Ferris. Said 'e'd fetch 'er some time this morning, so if you were wanting to take 'er out later…'

As if sensing Tina's disappointment, Richard glanced at her and suggested, 'If you fancy a ride now, Jupiter will easily take both of us.'

At her eager acceptance, he nodded to the groom. 'Saddle him up, Josh.'

As soon as the horse was ready, the groom disappeared, to return almost immediately with two riding hats.

'There be yours, Mr Richard, and I fancy the mistress's old un'll do fine for Miss Dunbar.'

The protective headgear buckled into place, Tina climbed the two steps to the mounting block and in a trice was astride Jupiter's broad back, taking care to leave the stirrups free for Richard.

He swung himself lightly into the saddle behind her and a moment later, with a wave to Josh, they were off.

Holding the reins in his left hand, his right arm securely around Tina, for a while they ambled along, heading south through pleasant undulating parkland.

After they had gone some half a mile, in response to Jupiter's urging, Richard gave the beast his head and, making light of his load, the big horse broke into an easy canter.

It was exhilarating and Tina laughed aloud with the sheer joy of it. In response to such spontaneous gladness, Richard's arm tightened around her.

When a shallow stream came into view, unwilling to overtax the horse, he reined him in and they ambled down to the water's edge.

There, where the grass was still green and lush and the trees made a dappled shade, he slid to the ground and, having lifted Tina down, looped the reins over a low branch.

Then, leaving the horse to graze peacefully, they took off their riding hats and went to sit on a fallen tree trunk by the fast-flowing stream.

Held in the crook of Richard's arm, Tina watched the glittering water as it ran leaping and chuckling over its stony bed and knew what perfect happiness and contentment felt like.

After a while he broke the silence to say, 'I'd like us to be married as soon as possible.'

When something in his tone, a kind of tension, made her glance up at him, he added almost roughly, 'I sound impatient, I know, but I just can't wait to make you mine.'

Her heart fluttered and swelled with gratitude that he should feel so strongly about her.

'If you were hoping for a big wedding with dozens of guests and all the trimmings,' he went on, 'we can always have a second ceremony later.'

Nestling against him, she said simply, 'I don't need a big wedding and all the trimmings,' and heard his quick sigh of relief.

'That's my girl.' His arm tightened round her. 'So shall we say tomorrow morning?'

Thinking he was joking, she laughed and said, 'Why not? Except that it can't be done so quickly.'

'As we have our own priest and our own chapel, all we need to do is warn the Reverend Peter and arrange for two witnesses.'

Realising he wasn't joking after all, she said breathlessly, 'B-but surely we need a…a licence of some kind?'

'I have a special licence lined up.'

Through lips gone suddenly stiff, she said, 'Then you must have intended it for someone else.'

'You are the only woman I've ever wanted to marry.' His green-gold eyes on her face, he added, 'I told you earlier that the first time I saw you I knew you were the one I'd been waiting for.'

She half shook her head. 'I realise that being who you are, you must have quite a pull. But, even with your own chapel and your own family priest, I don't believe you could have got a licence in the time. You hadn't set eyes on me until Friday…'

'That's where you're wrong,' he told her quietly.

CHAPTER EIGHT

'I DON'T understand,' Tina protested, puzzled.

Richard brushed a strand of silky blonde hair away from her cheek with his free hand and said, 'It's over three weeks since I first saw you.'

'Three weeks?'

'I was visiting Cartel Wines when I caught sight of you coming out of De Vere's office. I thought you were the most beautiful woman I'd ever seen and I knew I had to have you…'

She was still endeavouring to catch her breath when he went on, 'Unfortunately, the following day I was forced to travel to the Far East on an extremely important business trip, so I couldn't follow things through myself.

'However, I had some checks made and, finding you were free, I discussed getting married with the Reverend Peter, who made all the necessary arrangements—'

Completely flabbergasted, she protested, 'But you hadn't even spoken to me. How could you be so sure I'd marry you?'

'I couldn't be *sure*, of course…' With a trace of arrogance, he added, 'But I usually get what I want.'

She could easily believe it. Especially when it came to women.

'The trip dragged on until the middle of last week,' he continued, 'but for the first time in my life I found I couldn't keep my mind on business matters. I kept thinking about you, planning how to meet you when I got back.'

'And then we met by accident…' But, even as she said the words, some sixth sense made her wonder—*had* running into her been an accident?

Oh, don't be a fool, she chided herself. What man in his right mind would do such a thing deliberately when there were plenty of other ways he could have met her?

For instance, if he'd wanted to get to know her so badly, why hadn't he spoken to her in the car park at midday, while she had been disposing of her ruined lunch? It would have been a perfect opportunity.

Or, failing that, surely the next time he visited Cartel Wines he could have made some excuse to—

No, she wouldn't have been there.

Though he couldn't have known that she was leaving.

Or could he?

Somewhere at the back of her mind, a memory, an impression, tried to struggle to the surface and she knew that if she could only recall what it was she would have the answer to her question.

She was still cudgelling her brains when Richard glanced at his watch and said briskly, 'We ought to be starting for home. You must be famished and, as we're being married tomorrow, we have a lot to do.'

Though she wanted to marry him more than anything in the world, a vague uneasiness still nagging at her, a feeling that something wasn't quite right, she began, 'I don't understand why we have to rush into it like this… Couldn't we wait until—?'

Just for an instant his beautiful mouth tightened. Then he said coaxingly, 'You've agreed to marry me, we have a priest, a chapel and a marriage licence, so why wait?'

'I've nothing to wear,' she pointed out. 'I need to go back to the flat and fetch some clothes—'

He bent his dark head and kissed her mouth, nipping delicately at her bottom lip, distracting her, as he whispered, 'I'd rather have you without any clothes.'

Trying to collect herself and sound severe, she began, 'That's all very well, but I must have *something* to get married in—'

'Failing anything else, you could always wear the dress you wore to dinner last night.'

'But it got marked when we walked though the tunnel,' she pleaded.

'I'll ask Hannah to see that all your things are laundered and we'll make time to buy you a whole new wardrobe before we go on our honeymoon.'

Diverted, she asked, 'Are we going on honeymoon?'

He looked surprised. 'Of course. I thought we'd stick with the old tradition of spending our wedding night at Anders, in the nuptial bed…'

The nuptial bed… A little shiver of excitement ran down her spine.

'Then go on to our chosen honeymoon destination the following day.'

It all sounded so *solid*, so conventional, that, her uneasiness taking flight, she teased, 'I dare say you've already got it all arranged?'

He grinned appreciatively. ''Fraid not. I decided to find out where you wanted to go before I made any definite plans.'

'How long will we be going for?'

'A month. Longer if you wish…'

There was no harm in delaying the showdown; in fact it might be all to the good to allow a breathing space while they really got to know one other.

'So, if you'd like to give it some thought and let me know,' he added, 'I'll have Murray standing by.'

'Murray?'

'Captain Murray Tyler. I have a small private jet.'

That casual mention of owning his own plane made Tina

realise afresh what a wealthy man she was marrying. But it wasn't his money or his lifestyle that had attracted her. She would still have married him if he hadn't had a penny.

'We'd best be moving.' He stood up and, taking her hands, pulled her to her feet. 'Matthew Caradine, my solicitor, is coming at two o'clock.'

Surprised, she said, 'On a Sunday?'

'There are one or two things that need to be settled before tomorrow,' he told her casually.

When they had both donned their riding hats, he lifted her into the saddle, swung himself up behind her and a moment later they were heading for home at a canter.

Admittedly it hadn't been quite as easy as he might have hoped, but he had achieved what he'd set out to achieve. Tomorrow he would be her husband; he would be in a much stronger position once she'd signed the marriage contract that Matthew Caradine had drawn up.

When lunch was over Richard asked for coffee to be served in their suite and, an arm around Tina's waist, escorted her up the stairs.

Once their coffee cups were empty, he said seriously, 'When we get married I shall use the wedding ring my mother bought my father...'

Knowing that some men preferred to hide the fact that they were married, Tina was only too pleased that Richard wasn't one of them.

'Until we have time to go and choose *your* rings,' he was going on, 'I'd like you to use my mother's. If you're quite happy with that?'

'Are you sure she wouldn't have minded?'

'I'm certain. It was her stated intention to give her rings to my future wife—should she want them, that is.'

A warm feeling spreading inside, Tina assured him, 'Then, if they fit, I'd love to wear them.'

'Of course I'm talking about the rings my father bought her. Bradley, who apparently was very jealous, hated to see her wearing them, so when they were married she took them off and kept them in her secret drawer along with my father's wedding ring…'

He went over to the writing desk where, placed centrally above several small drawers faced with oyster shell and inlaid with box, their handles made of mother-of-pearl, was a shallow recess.

Tina watched with undisguised interest as, a hand at either end, he reached into the space and a moment later what had appeared to be a solid back slid forward to reveal a drawer some thirty centimetres long, twenty wide and ten deep.

From it he took a small box covered in dark blue velvet and flicked open the lid to show a heavy gold signet ring, a delicate chased gold wedding band and an exquisite matching diamond solitaire.

'Her fingers were very slim, like yours, so I think they'll fit.'

He took out the solitaire and, lifting Tina's strong but slender left hand with its pearly oval nails, slid it on to the fourth finger.

It fitted perfectly and she caught her breath as the huge stone flashed with internal fire.

Nodding his approval, Richard replaced the box containing both the wedding rings and sent the secret drawer sliding back into the recess. It seemed to catch slightly before finally settling into place.

The long-case clock in the corner was just striking two o'clock and at that instant Milly tapped at the door to announce that the solicitor had arrived.

'Coming?' Richard cocked an eyebrow at Tina.

'I thought I'd stay here while you—'

He shook his head firmly. 'There's one thing that concerns you.'

'What kind of thing?' she asked as they made their way back downstairs.

'We need to agree on a suitable settlement in the event of a divorce.'

A cold chill ran down her spine. 'Oh, but I—'

Seeing that involuntary shiver, he said reassuringly, 'Don't worry, it's just a formality. But it's something that has to be gone through.'

The solicitor was waiting in the study. Almost as tall as Richard but a good deal heavier, he was a pleasant-looking middle-aged man with greying hair and jowls.

'Good of you to come at such short notice,' Richard said as the two men shook hands.

He turned to Tina and, drawing her forward, went on, 'Darling, this is Matthew Caradine... Matthew, my fiancée, Valentina Dunbar.'

The solicitor took Tina's proffered hand with a friendly smile and said, 'It's nice to meet you, Miss Dunbar...'

Then, to Richard, 'I've drawn up the necessary documents to cover all the points you mentioned.'

'Good.'

'There's really only the one pertaining to your marriage that concerns Miss Dunbar and, as you requested, I've kept it simple. So, if you'd like to get that out of the way first?'

At Richard's nod he opened his black briefcase and, taking out a single sheet of paper, handed it to Tina. 'Perhaps you'd be good enough to read that and, if you're satisfied with the contents, sign it?'

She took the document and, sitting down in one of the armchairs, proceeded to read it while the two men stood and watched her in silence.

It was, as the solicitor had said, short and simple. It stated that if, for whatever reason, they were divorced, while Richard would be happy to buy her a house and pay her maintenance—

the amount was so generous it made her blink—she had to relinquish any claim to the castle.

It further stated that if there were children from the marriage,
in the event of a separation, their father would be responsible
for their upbringing and they would remain in his care.

Having read it through twice, she put it down on the coffee
table and said flatly, 'I'm sorry, but I can't sign this.'

She saw Richard's jaw tighten and a white line appear
round his mouth.

It was a moment before he asked evenly, 'Why not?'

'With regard to the castle…' she began.

For a split second he looked so angry that she cringed
inwardly and the words died on her lips.

Then that look was gone and, his voice quiet and controlled,
he queried, 'What about the castle?'

'I—I was just going to say that there's no question that it
belongs to you. I would never dream of—'

She glimpsed what might have been relief, before he broke
in, 'So what exactly is the problem?'

Well aware that he might not marry her if she refused to toe
the line, she took a deep breath and told him, 'There's no way
I would be prepared to give up my children…'

A flicker of some emotion she was unable to decipher
crossed his face before he said, 'Then perhaps we could agree
on joint custody?'

'How do you mean, exactly?'

'I mean that if we separated, they could live with you but I
would have unlimited access and an equal right to a say in their
upbringing. Would you be happy with that arrangement?'

'Yes,' she said simply. 'Though I hope it will never come to
that.'

He took her hand and raised it to his lips. 'With you as my
wife, I'm sure it won't.'

Caradine came forward and, picking up the document, sat

down at the desk. 'As you're both in agreement, I'll amend it immediately.'

The amendment completed, he suggested, 'If you'd both be good enough to read it and put your signatures at the bottom?'

That done to his satisfaction, he replaced the paper in his briefcase and took out several more. 'Now, for the remainder of the business…'

Tina got to her feet. 'If you don't need me any longer, I'll go and leave you to it.'

A detaining hand on her arm, Richard asked, 'What were you thinking of doing?'

A little surprised by the barely concealed urgency of his manner, she said, 'It's such a lovely day I thought I might go for a stroll along the battlements and enjoy the view.'

His fingers relaxed their grip and, dropping a light kiss on her lips, he said, 'What a good idea… While you're up there, give some thought to our honeymoon. Try and decide where you'd like to go and what you'd like to see…

'By the time you've gone full circle,' he added, 'I should be finished here. Then, after I've seen Matthew off, we can go and talk to the Reverend Peter and make some precise arrangements for tomorrow.'

She smiled and nodded, then thanked the solicitor and shook hands with him, before going out and closing the door quietly behind her.

Having crossed the deserted hall, where the sun threw elaborate patterns of the leaded windows on to the polished oak floorboards, she made her way to the tower they had ascended the previous evening and climbed the stone stairway.

Emerging on to the castle walls, she paused to look down into the courtyard, which was asymmetrically painted with deep shadows and bright sunshine. A sleek blue Jaguar, no doubt Matthew Caradine's, was drawn up by the main entrance.

Though Richard had tried hard to get her to focus on their

wedding day and honeymoon, as she began to walk slowly along the sunny battlements, her mind went back over the past half hour and the little scene that had taken place in his study.

Why had he deemed it necessary to insist that she should relinquish any claim to the castle?

And why had he been so angry when he'd thought that she was refusing to? Because, clearly, that was what he *had* thought.

Which was absurd.

Even if she'd wanted to, which she never would, how could she possibly lay claim to something that had belonged to his family for generations?

Giving up the puzzle for the time being, she moved at a leisurely pace, simply enjoying the view and the fresh air, the warmth of the sunshine,

She had almost completed the circuit when she became aware of something hovering on the edge of her consciousness. Something nebulous and insubstantial, yet oddly persistent.

Instinctively she knew that it was the same thing that had troubled her that morning as she'd sat by the river with Richard.

After struggling, and once again failing, to identify it, she realised that it was useless to rack her brains and gave up trying.

No doubt it would crystallize eventually.

A glance down into the courtyard below showed that the solicitor's Jaguar had disappeared, but there was no sign of Richard.

Thinking he might have returned to his study, she made her way there and put her head round the door. Though there were still papers spread on the desk, the room was empty.

As she turned to leave, she noticed the file she had knocked off the desk that morning and paused as a fleeting picture, an image she couldn't pin down, came into her mind, convincing her that *that* held the answer to whatever had been troubling her.

She went in, leaving the door ajar, and opened the file.

It contained various emails and papers that Richard had

roughly gathered together, along with a brown envelope from which some photographs were protruding.

The top one showed part of a woman's face, which looked oddly familiar. Curiosity having prompted Tina to pull it out and take a better look, she found she was staring down at a very good likeness of herself.

There were several more, all taken—judging by the background—at Cartel Wines, and all taken without her knowledge.

She felt uncomfortable, exposed, spied on.

But, even as she stared at them, she knew that the photographs weren't the solution to what had been niggling at her.

A second or two later, catching sight of a logo on one of the papers, she had her answer. *That* was what she had glimpsed earlier in the morning and subconsciously registered.

It was a stylized representation of a mountain that she recognised as the distinctive shape of the Matterhorn.

She was still gazing down at it, her mind racing, when the door was pushed open and Richard walked in.

'I'm sorry if I've kept you waiting. I was just seeing Caradine off when Hannah told me that the new Estate Manager wanted a word—'

Noticing the open file, he stopped speaking abruptly and his eyes caught and held hers.

Knowing she couldn't really justify her prying, Tina's eyes were the first to drop.

'Find what you were looking for?' he enquired sardonically.

'As a matter of fact, I did.' Then, taking the bull by the horns, she asked bluntly, 'What exactly is your connection with the Matterhorn group?'

Just as bluntly he answered, 'I own it.'

So that explained his presence at Cartel Wines.

Gathering herself, she challenged, 'When I talked about Cartel Wines being taken over by Matterhorn, you didn't tell me you owned it.'

'No,' he agreed calmly.

'Why didn't you?' she persisted.

'After you'd just lost your job because of the takeover, it didn't seem to be quite the right time,' he answered quizzically.

'Well, I still think you should have told me.'

'What difference would it have made?'

None really, she admitted silently. It wasn't as if he'd been *trying* to hide the fact that he owned the Matterhorn group. Once she had asked him, he'd answered without a moment's hesitation.

So why did she feel as if she'd been bamboozled, as if he'd been deliberately keeping it from her?

But what possible reason could he have had for not telling her?

After a moment she recalled the doubts that had entered her mind that morning as they'd sat by the river bank.

Suppose the accident *hadn't* been an accident? Suppose, on returning from his business trip and visiting Cartel Wines, he'd discovered that she was leaving that evening for good. Could he have thought it urgent enough to stage an 'accident' so he could get to know her?

No, surely not.

For one thing, in the pitch-dark he couldn't have known who he was running into.

Unless he'd been following her. Keeping an eye on her. Recalling that disturbing sensation of being watched, she shivered.

No, she was just being ridiculous. If he *had* discovered at the last minute that she was leaving, all he would have needed to do was make himself known and offer her a place on the new team. That way he would have had all the time in the world to get to know her.

So why on earth should he need to take such drastic action? It didn't make sense.

All the same, she found herself saying accusingly, 'You knew I was leaving Cartel Wines that night.'

'You told me,' he pointed out.

'You must have known before that.'

He lifted a dark brow. 'Why must I have known?'

'As Matterhorn's boss you must have been aware that having your own promotional team would make the job I do redundant.'

Patiently, as though speaking to a not-very-bright child, he pointed out, 'As Matterhorn's boss, I only keep hold of the reins and make the executive decisions. I just don't have time to get involved with the ins and outs of company policy, or the day-to-day running of things. That's what I employ managers for.'

Feeling silly, she said, 'Of course… I'm sorry.'

What on earth had she been thinking of? she berated herself. Naturally the big boss wouldn't be au fait with minor details.

It was high time she pulled herself together and stopped letting her imagination run away with her.

But she hadn't imagined the photographs.

As though he'd read that searing thought, he remarked casually, 'I see you've come across your photographs.'

Taken aback by his cool nonchalance, she asked unsteadily, 'Why did you take them?'

'I didn't.'

'Then who did, and why?'

'If you remember, I mentioned earlier that just after I'd first seen you, and while I was still reeling from finding the woman I'd been waiting for, I had to go away on a business trip…

'At that point, all I knew about you was your name and the fact that you were working for Cartel Wines. Two things De Vere had grudgingly admitted when I'd asked him who you were.

'I wanted to know a whole lot more so, before I went away, I hired a detective to find out as much as he could about you. *He* took the photographs.'

The thought of being kept under surveillance and photographed without her knowledge was far from pleasant, and she said so.

'Yes, I'm sorry I had to resort to that. But I needed to know, and in the circumstances…'

Honestly puzzled, she protested, 'I don't understand why you were in such a hurry, why you couldn't have waited. Even if I'd left Cartel Wines, the personnel department had my address; you could have—'

'Call me impetuous.' Pulling her into his arms, he began to kiss her deeply, his ardour sweeping her away, swamping any further attempt at logical thought or protest.

She was limp and quivering all over by the time he released her lips and, putting his cheek to hers, whispered in her ear, 'Shall we go upstairs…?'

Though she was sorely tempted, a sense of what was fitting made her say a little breathlessly, 'But suppose someone wants you?'

He kissed the warm hollow behind her ear before nibbling the lobe. 'I rather hoped *you* would.'

Feeling her resolve beginning to slip away, she said hastily, 'What about the Reverend Peter? Don't we need to talk to him?'

'You're quite right, we do… What a very practical woman you are… Ah, well, once all the arrangements have been finalized we can give each other our undivided attention.'

Rubbing his cheek against hers, he asked seductively, 'Have you ever made love in the open air with the sun pouring down and a gentle breeze caressing your skin?'

'No,' she whispered.

'Then it's high time you did. It adds a whole new dimension. After we've talked to the Reverend Peter, I propose that we go for a stroll.'

His voice deepening, he added, 'On the far side of the beechwood there's a sunny and secluded little clearing that's ideal…'

The words tailed off as his lips moved down the side of her neck, making her shiver deliciously, and his fingers undid the top two buttons of her silk shirt and slipped inside to fondle her breast.

Though it took all her willpower, disliking the thought of facing the priest looking all hot and bothered, she made a muffled protest.

With a sigh, Richard reluctantly removed his hand and, pulling the front of her shirt together, refastened the buttons.

'No wonder newly married couples go away on honeymoon,' he said wryly. 'For that length of time, at least, they can forget everything and lose themselves in each other.

'And, speaking of honeymoons, have you decided where you'd like to go on yours?'

'I don't mind in the slightest,' she said happily. 'I'll leave it to you.' Anywhere on earth would be heaven so long as he was there.

'Come along then, my love.'

So she really was his love... Her heart soared like a bird.

As, hand in hand, they made their way to the priest's quarters, which adjoined the little chapel, Richard said, 'I'd prefer the ceremony to take place in the morning. Unless you have any objections?'

She shook her head. 'If that's what you want.'

'Then shall we say ten o'clock? That way, when we've had lunch we can go into Anders Cross and shop for a trousseau...'

If they shopped in the morning and got married in the afternoon, she could have a new dress to be married in.

She had opened her mouth to point that out when something...pride? Pique?...made her bite back the words.

He was the one who was calling the tune and perhaps, manlike, he simply wasn't interested in clothes.

So if it didn't matter to him that she had nothing to wear, perhaps he was just plain insensitive and didn't realise that it *did* matter to her.

But he was going on, 'There are several good little boutiques and a branch of Bertolli's Fashion House if you like his designs?'

Taking a deep breath, she said evenly, 'Yes, I do.'

And it was true. She had always admired Bertolli's classical collections, though until now they had been way out of her price range. It would seem strange to be able to choose a new wardrobe without having to worry about the cost.

As they approached the priest's quarters he emerged from the door and came to greet them.

He was a short, tubby man with a jolly face and a fringe of pure white hair surrounding a large bald spot that reminded Tina of a monk's tonsure.

She was forced to stifle a chuckle when Richard leaned closer and said, *sotto voce*, 'Put him in a habit and you've got Friar Tuck.'

After the introductions had been made, beaming, he shepherded them into the chapel, which appeared dim after the brightness of the sunshine.

When her eyes adjusted to the gloom, Tina glanced around her. To one side of a simple altar, with a plain gold cross and twin candles, a short flight of wooden steps with a curving handrail led up to a small, intricately carved pulpit.

A lectern in the form of a brass eagle with spread wings held a large black Bible and either side of the chancel steps a tall flower arrangement added colour and scented the air.

At the rear was a screened organ and a stone font, while a dozen well-polished pews that smelled of beeswax and lavender took up most of the floor space. Shafts of sunshine slanting through the stained glass windows threw jewelled patterns across the backs of the pews and the red carpet that ran down the central aisle.

Tina sighed. It was beautiful and tranquil, a lovely place to be married in.

As though in response to that thought, Richard's fingers tightened on hers and, her pique forgotten, her heart swelled with love and gratitude.

When the arrangements had been discussed and settled on, the Reverend Peter turned to Richard and remarked, 'I'm delighted you've decided to use your parents' rings. I know it would have made your mother very happy.

'Oh, and speaking of your mother, I've been thinking about the second will that Hannah and I witnessed…'

Apparently not noticing the warning look that Richard gave him, the cleric went on, 'It occurred to me that it might have got mixed up with some of the ecclesiastical papers that she was going through at the time, so if you could spare a few minutes to—'

'I'd prefer to make it later,' Richard broke in. Putting an arm around Tina's waist, he explained, 'We were just about to take a walk.'

'If you've something to deal with, I can always start walking and you can follow on when you're ready,' she suggested practically.

His face clearing, he asked, 'Sure you don't mind?'

'Of course not.'

'Then if you take the path round the moat and head for the beechwood, I'll catch you up.'

He bent his dark head and kissed her, the promise explicit in that kiss taking her breath away and making her heart beat faster.

A little flushed, she thanked the cleric and said goodbye, before leaving the chapel.

When she got outside, the engagement ring she wore caught the sun and sparkled brilliantly. Imagining Ruth's face when she saw it, Tina smiled to herself.

Which reminded her, Ruth would be expecting her back on Monday, so she must ring the flat later and let the other girl know what was happening.

When she reached the bridge she leaned her arms on the old creeper-covered parapet and dawdled for a while, looking at the pleasant scene.

Fluffy white clouds hung in the deep blue sky and, along with tall feathery reeds and grey stone walls, were reflected in the still waters of the moat. Then a paddle of ducks came swimming busily along, breaking the smooth picture into a series of ripples.

Beneath the surface, she could see huge golden carp moving idly and a water rat, sleek and streamlined, surfaced briefly before disappearing into a hole in the bank.

When some fifteen minutes had passed and there was no sign of Richard, she set off to stroll round the moat. After she had gone a little way it occurred to her that she was walking widdershins and she hoped it wasn't unlucky.

After a while she glanced back and, finding Richard was still nowhere in sight, she decided to sit down and wait.

All the cottonwool clouds had vanished now and the sun, low in a sky the colour of forget-me-nots, was bathing the parkland and the individual trees in a low golden light that cast long blue-black shadows across the turf.

Lack of sleep the previous night and the warmth of the dying sun on her face combined to make her feel soporific and, stretching out on the grass, her head pillowed on a handy tussock, she closed her eyes.

She was drifting, half asleep and half awake, when she heard the sound of a horse's hooves.

Sitting up, she looked around, half expecting to see Richard had changed his mind about walking and had brought Jupiter.

But the rider who was approaching was a woman on a bay mare. A woman she recognised as Helen O'Connell.

CHAPTER NINE

THE newcomer dismounted and, leaving the mare, which began to graze quietly, crossed to where Tina was sitting and sat down beside her.

She was dressed in jodhpurs and a well-tailored riding jacket. Pulling off her riding hat, she put it on the grass beside her and said without preamble, 'My name's Helen O'Connell…'

At close quarters Tina could see that the newcomer was somewhere in her early thirties, with glossy dark hair, big blue eyes and a smooth, creamy skin.

Her eyes fixed on the sparkling solitaire that Tina wore, she said, 'You must be Valentina Dunbar, the woman Richard's planning to marry. When I caught sight of you I decided to take the chance to talk to you. When is this wedding supposed to take place?'

Trying not to let the other woman's abrupt manner throw her, Tina answered, 'Tomorrow morning.'

Helen laughed bitterly. 'I have to hand it to him. He said there was no time to lose, but I didn't think he could bring it off so soon.

'And when you're safely married he's planning to take you away on a nice little honeymoon, I imagine?'

'Well, yes, but I really don't see—'

'Let me give you a word of warning. Don't go ahead with

the wedding whatever you do. If you marry him you'll find you've made a serious mistake.'

Before Tina could speak, she hurried on, 'I know he's a very wealthy man, but—'

'I'm not marrying him for his money.'

Helen glanced at her sharply. 'Well, all I can say is if you've fallen for him you have my sympathy. He doesn't care a jot about you.

'I don't suppose he's told you—it wouldn't pay him to—but he and I have been lovers for years and if all this trouble hadn't blown up he would have married me.'

'I'm sorry,' Tina began helplessly, 'but I—'

'Oh, I don't blame *you*,' Helen broke in. 'As far as I'm concerned, *you're* the innocent party. It's Richard who, for once in his life, is behaving like a fool. He seems to think that marrying you is the only way.

'But don't let yourself be conned; as soon as he's got what he wants and the honeymoon's over, he'll divorce you—' She broke off abruptly as, in the distance, a tall figure came into view.

Springing to her feet, she pulled on her riding hat and re-mounted the mare.

'Believe me, you'll be a lot better off if you don't listen to a word Richard says. Just pack your bags and go.' Clapping her heels to the animal's flanks, she galloped away.

Thrown totally off balance, her mind in a whirl, Tina was still sitting staring after her when Richard came striding up, his good-looking face tense.

Dropping down beside her on the grass, he asked, 'What's wrong? You look like a ghost.'

'Nothing's wrong. I—'

'Don't lie to me,' he broke in curtly. 'I saw Helen ride off. What's she been saying to you?'

Struggling to keep her voice steady, Tina admitted, 'She warned me not to marry you.'

Mentally cursing Helen and her meddling, he demanded, 'Did she give you any reason for saying such a thing?'

Tina shook her head. 'She just said I'd be making a serious mistake.'

'What else did she say?'

'That you didn't care a jot about me. That you and she have been lovers for years…'

'Go on,' he ordered tersely.

'There's not a great deal more.'

His voice inexorable, he repeated, 'Go on.'

Tina looked down at her hands shyly. 'She said, "He seems to think that marrying you is the only way. But don't let yourself be conned; as soon as he's got what he wants…he'll divorce you".'

'I see,' he said grimly. 'Well, I hope you don't believe any of that nonsense.'

When she stayed silent, he sighed. 'I see you do.'

'I don't know what to believe,' Tina admitted helplessly. 'It doesn't make any sense, but why should she say something like that if it isn't—?'

He smirked. 'Try jealousy.'

'Then it's true that you and she are lovers?'

'It's true that we have been,' he admitted. 'But that's all in the past. Though we're still good friends, as far as I'm concerned anything more ended a long time ago.'

'Then you're not still in love with her?'

'I was never in love with her. Nor she with me. It was just a light-hearted affair that suited us both. A temporary thing with no serious future.'

'*She* doesn't seem to think so,' Tina said flatly. 'She said that if all this trouble hadn't blown up you would have married her.'

'But she didn't say what "all this trouble" was?' he asked quickly.

Tina shook her head again. 'No, she didn't.'

A flicker of emotion crossed his face but was quickly hidden before he went on, 'Probably something she invented. I'm sorry to say that she's prone to fancies.

'And, as for marrying her, that's another thing she must have dreamt up. At no time have I ever considered making her my wife.'

Seeing Tina's quick glance, he added firmly, 'Nor have I ever given her the slightest reason to think that I would. Now stop worrying over Helen's jealous nonsense. It's *you* I love. *You* I want to marry.'

Putting an arm around her shoulders, he drew her close and turned her face up to his. 'I hope that sets your mind at rest.'

But her mind, buzzing with doubts and questions, was anything but at rest and when he leaned forward to kiss her she tensed.

After a moment or two, however, as his mouth worked its magic, she relaxed and let all the doubts and unanswered questions slip away. Richard was here by her side. He loved her and he wanted to marry her. Why let another woman's jealousy spoil her happiness?

By the time he had seduced her with his kisses, though the sun was now slipping below the horizon and a little breeze had sprung up, she would still have gone with him to the beechwood, had he asked.

But when, released from the shelter of his arms, she shivered, he noticed at once and said, 'Straight home, I think.'

With a rueful sigh, he added, 'Due to my tardiness it'll soon be dusk and it can turn cool quickly at this time of the year.'

Rising to his feet and holding out a strong right hand to pull her up, he added, 'I admit that a bed lacks that alfresco touch, but being comfortable and warm does have its advantages.'

Wanting to keep her mind off Helen's unforeseen—and potentially disastrous—intervention, he went on, 'And of course our bed is centuries old, which makes it somewhat special...'

Thrilled at the *our bed*, she said, 'You called it the nuptial bed...'

'Yes, apart from Mother and Bradley—who went straight

away on honeymoon—for generations the master and his bride have spent their wedding night in it. If it were able to talk, I imagine it could tell some tales…'

As they started to walk back, his fingers entwined in hers, he said, 'Part of a piece of poetry by the Scottish poet, James Thomson sums it up nicely:

> *"And while the black night nothing saw,*
> *And till the cold morn came at last,*
> *That old bed held the room in awe*
> *With tales of its experience vast.*
> *It thrilled the gloom; it told such tales*
> *Of human sorrows and delights,*
> *Of fever moans and infant wails,*
> *Of births and deaths and bridal nights".'*

He had an attractive voice and she listened, enthralled. When he'd finished, she said, 'I see what you mean.' Then, 'Do you like poetry?'

Picking up the surprise she had failed to hide, he laughed. 'You sound as if you think liking poetry is in some way effeminate.'

'No, of course I don't. I just hadn't put you down as someone who would…' The words tailed off.

As though afraid of spoiling his macho image, Kevin had frequently decried poetry as being only for women or sissies.

'But in answer to your question,' Richard went on, 'yes, I like poetry. Mainly the classical stuff. People like Marvell and Donne. How about you?'

For the rest of the way back they discussed poetry.

When they reached the castle, the housekeeper appeared in the hall and beamed at them both, before addressing Richard. 'The Reverend Peter mentioned that the wedding ceremony will be taking place tomorrow morning.'

'That's right.'

'Cook and I will be pleased to organise a wedding breakfast, if you can give me some idea of numbers?'

'As I intend to keep things quiet and private, only ourselves, the indoor staff and the estate workers.

'Later, when we return from our honeymoon, I hope to have another ceremony, with guests, a reception and all the trimmings.'

Hannah smiled and nodded, before saying, 'All the things you asked for have been delivered and are waiting in your suite.

'Signora Diomede, who brought them over personally, asked me to say that should there be the slightest problem, if you give her a ring she'll sort it out.'

Turning to Tina, she went on, 'If you would like some help dressing tomorrow, please let me know.'

Visualizing her simple blue sheath, Tina said, 'Thank you, Hannah, but I really don't think I'll need any help.'

Hannah nodded. 'As you wish. Now, would you like tea served in the downstairs sitting-room, Mr Richard, or in your suite? As it seems to have turned appreciably cooler, I've had all the fires lit.'

'Then we'll have tea upstairs, please, Hannah.'

When they reached the suite, a blue dusk was pressing against the leaded panes while a log fire blazed cheerfully in the grate.

They had just settled themselves on the couch in front of it, when Milly arrived with the tea tray and put it down on a low table before giving a little bob and departing.

Along with the tea were some muffins, a large pat of butter and a bowl of clear golden honey and a long-handled toasting fork.

'Shall I toast the muffins?' Richard asked, 'or would you like to join in the fun?'

'I'd like to join in,' Tina answered without hesitation. 'I haven't toasted a muffin since I was a child and though, to be honest, I nearly always burnt them, I used to love it.'

Amused by her enthusiasm, he handed her the toasting fork and said, 'Right, you can do the first two, I'll do the second.'

Spearing a muffin, she knelt down in front of the blaze and, a little frown of concentration furrowing her forehead, set to work.

He watched the flames flickering on her lovely profile and her cheeks growing pink from the heat when she turned her head to smile at him. He was filled with a sudden fierce, all-consuming anger that made him want to smash his fist against something and rage against fate.

Although he was well aware that she wasn't the sweet innocent she seemed, he knew without a shadow of a doubt that she was the woman he'd been waiting for. The only woman who had ever got under his skin and into his blood.

In addition, he was starting to appreciate that, as well as outward beauty, she had an inner strength, a mind of a curiously tough quality that stimulated his own. And, perhaps most important of all, an *integrity* that made him wonder if he shouldn't have chosen one of the other options.

But, despite the fact that so much hung in the balance, he could only go forward. It was far too late to alter his plans…

'There!' she said triumphantly. 'Two perfectly toasted muffins…'

Having admired the golden buns, he said quizzically, 'I can see that when it's my turn I've got a lot to live up to.'

When the tea had been drunk and the last of the muffins eaten, Tina sighed contentedly and with the end of a pink tongue licked a dribble of honey from her index finger. 'I won't need anything else to eat for a week.'

His white teeth gleamed as he laughed. 'At the moment I feel much the same, so it's just as well we settled on an eight o'clock dinner. I dare say by then we'll both have changed our minds.'

Having moved the tea things out of the way, he crossed to one of the occasional tables and, picking up a small pile of midnight-blue boxes, dropped them on to the couch beside her.

'In the meantime, suppose you open your things?'

'My things?' she exclaimed. 'But I thought you said we'd shop for a trousseau tomorrow afternoon.'

'And so we will. However, you need something to be married in.'

Taking a seat in one of the armchairs, he watched her face and heard her catch her breath as she untied the silver ribbon and lifted the first lid.

Inside, enfolded in the finest tissue paper, was a beautiful ivory silk wedding gown, with a medieval-style neckline and sleeves. A discreet label stated that it was designed by Bertolli.

Accompanying it was a rhinestone coronet, a gossamer veil, matching shoes, sheer silk stockings and delicate underwear.

Everything a bride could need, and all things she would have chosen herself.

How could she have suspected him of being insensitive?

She looked up, her eyes swimming with tears, and said simply, 'Thank you.'

'I hope you like the dress.'

'Oh, I do.' As, impulsively, she went over to him and stooped to kiss him, a single bright tear escaped and rolled down her cheek.

He made an inarticulate sound and, pulling her on to his knee, kissed it away before finding her mouth once more.

When finally he reluctantly freed her lips, she said huskily, 'I don't understand how you managed to get it on a Sunday.'

'Apart from the fact that I have a financial interest in Bertolli's, Signora Diomede, the head of that particular branch, is a friend of mine, so it was easy. All I needed to do was phone and tell her your size and what I wanted.

'Unfortunately, because it was such short notice, it had to be a dress that was already in stock, but—'

Tina put a slim finger to his lips. 'Don't say *unfortunately*. I couldn't have wished for anything lovelier, truly.'

He looked pleased, then, his hands at her waist, he lifted her to her feet and rose with her. 'Though I was fairly confident about your size, it might be as well to make sure it fits.'

Then, briskly, 'While you're trying things on I've a spot of business to catch up with. As soon as that's sorted I'll talk to Murray Tyler and start making the arrangements for our honeymoon.'

Dropping a light kiss on her lips, he turned to go. As he reached the door he paused to say, 'When I get back, we can give each other our undivided attention for the rest of the evening.'

But the mention of a honeymoon had broken the spell he had so successfully woven and once again she could hear Helen O'Connell's voice saying derisively, '…he's planning to take you away on a nice little honeymoon, I imagine?'

Doing her utmost to push the unpleasant memory away, Tina carried the packages through to her bedroom—where a neat pile of freshly laundered clothes awaited her—and, having unpacked the contents, tried them on.

But her heart was no longer in it and, though everything fitted perfectly and in a detached kind of way she knew she had never looked so beautiful, her happiness had dispersed like morning mist.

Remembering that disturbing little scene by the moat, she felt tense and anxious and, as she took off her wedding dress and hung it up, she marvelled at how skilfully Richard had managed to take, and keep, her mind off it.

Until that fatal mention of a honeymoon.

Now all the doubts and questions were back, buzzing through her head, distracting and dangerous as a swarm of hornets.

What had Helen meant when she'd said, 'He seems to think that marrying you is the only way…'?

The only way to achieve *what*?

And then the even more disturbing, '…don't let yourself be conned; as soon as he's got what he wants and the honeymoon's over, he'll divorce you—'

Conned…that was a very emotive word…and *as soon as he's got what he wants*…

But what could he possibly want?

She was already sharing his bed and, compared to him, she was a mere nobody, with no money, no job and no background, so it just didn't add up.

If he *didn't* love her, but for some obscure reason he needed a wife, surely he could have married Helen?

Confused and agitated, trapped in a maze of doubts and conjectures, Tina was sitting by the fire still brooding over it when Richard returned.

It was nearly eight o'clock and as he came in he said apologetically, 'I'm sorry to have been so long, but my business took a lot more time than I'd anticipated.

'I take it you've tried your things—?' Catching sight of her face, he broke off to ask, 'What's the matter? Did I get the size wrong?'

A little jerkily, she assured him, 'No, no… everything's fine. The dress fits perfectly…'

'But you don't like it on?'

'Yes, I do. It looks lovely.'

'So what's the problem?'

For a moment she considered telling him and asking for answers to her questions, but almost instantly she dismissed the thought. Instinctively she knew he wouldn't give her any. He would dismiss the whole thing as nothing more than a jealous woman trying to make trouble.

Which perhaps it was.

Summoning a smile, she said, 'There is no problem.'

He came over and, tilting her face up to his, insisted, 'Sure?'

'Quite sure.'

But her blue-violet eyes were clouded and, guessing what was bothering her, he cursed Helen's interference afresh.

The moment he removed his hand and stepped back, she rose

to her feet and said hurriedly, 'I'd better see about getting showered and changed, otherwise I'll hold you up.'

She saw his mouth tighten, but he let her go without comment.

Dinner that night was a strained meal. Tina tried hard to appear her usual self and even managed to keep up a desultory conversation. But, uneasy and preoccupied, her head aching dully, she could scarcely eat a thing.

Watching her push her food round and round her plate, he remarked carefully, 'You don't appear to be eating much.'

A shade defensively, she said, 'It was a mistake to have two muffins.'

He said nothing further and she was relieved when, a little later, coffee was served.

When their cups were empty, he asked, 'What would you like to do for the rest of the evening?'

Feeling the need to be alone, she said, 'I'm rather tired. I'd like to have an early night.'

When she got to her feet, he rose with her. 'Not a bad idea.' Taking her hand, he studied her through long thick lashes. 'We could provide our bed with another tale to tell.'

She half shook her head.

He sighed. 'It's Helen, isn't it? I've told you not to take any notice of all that nonsense, but you're still worrying about it, aren't you?'

Knowing it was useless to discuss it, she denied, 'Not really.'

'Don't lie to me.'

Her throat desert-dry, her voice ragged, she said, 'I've got a headache.' Then, sensing his angry impatience, she stammered, 'I—I'm sorry, but I…'

'Don't worry, I subscribe to every woman's right to say no when she wants to.'

'I really do have a headache.'

'In that case I'll just hold you in my arms while you sleep.'

'I'd rather sleep alone,' she blurted out.

His jaw tightened before he said, 'Very well, if that's what you want, I'll say goodnight.'

He lifted her hand to his lips.

Chilled by that frigid courtesy, she mumbled, 'Goodnight,' and hurried upstairs.

Though it was true that she was tired, both physically and mentally, once in bed she was unable to sleep.

For what seemed an age she tossed and turned restlessly, plagued by unanswerable questions, her thoughts circling endlessly and always coming back to the same thing.

She had nothing to give Richard, apart from her love and a lifetime's commitment, so if he didn't love her, why was he so eager to marry her?

Surely he *must* love her, otherwise it didn't make any sense.

So why was she here alone? Why—she thought as she'd thought earlier—was she allowing another woman's jealousy to spoil her happiness?

Taking a deep breath, she got out of bed and, making her way to the master bedroom, opened the door quietly and slipped inside.

There were no lights burning, but in the glow from the dying fire she could see that Richard was lying flat on his back, his chest and shoulders bare, his hands clasped behind his dark head.

He was awake, she could see the gleam of his eyes in the semi-darkness as he turned his head to look at her, but he said nothing.

She quailed inwardly. Perhaps he was still angry at the way she had rejected him? Perhaps she was no longer welcome?

As she stood shivering, uncertain whether to go or stay, he reached out a hand.

When she slipped hers into it, he lifted the quilt and, still without a word, drew her into the bed and against the warmth of his naked body.

With a little sigh, she nestled against him, her head at the comfortable juncture between breastbone and shoulder, her hand flat on his chest.

The brush of fine body hair against her palm was both exciting and erotic and, feeling desire stir, she waited for him to make a move.

When he continued to lie there quite still, she realised he wasn't going to. She had pleaded a headache and he had taken her at her word. If she wanted to alter the scenario, *she* would have to make the running.

After a momentary hesitation she snuggled closer and, her fingers stroking over his smooth pectoral muscles, ran the sole of her foot up and down his hair-roughened leg.

When he continued to lie motionless, she let her hand slide over his ribcage and trim waist and down his flat stomach until it reached the crisp silkiness of hair.

All at once, his hand closed over hers and held it stationary. 'Be careful,' he warned softly. 'Don't tease unless you're prepared for the consequences.'

'Consequences?' she asked innocently.

'Yes, consequences.' He took his hand away.

Reminding herself that tomorrow he would be her husband, she did what she'd been longing to do and boldly let her fingers close around the warm firmness of his flesh.

She heard the breath hiss through his teeth before he remarked evenly, 'I thought you had a headache?'

'I did.'

'Does that mean it's gone?'

'Yes.'

'How convenient,' he said sarcastically.

She bit her lip and started to move away, but his arm tightened, pinning her there.

'Sorry, but it's too late to change your mind. I did warn you not to tease.'

'I wasn't teasing. At least not exactly... I—I wanted you to make love to me.'

'Wanted? Past tense?'

'I still do.'

'In that case...' With a sudden movement she was unprepared for, he turned and flipped her on to her back. 'Let me see what I can do to oblige.'

Suddenly scared of him in this mood, scared of what she had provoked, she whispered, 'Please, Richard.'

'Don't worry, I intend to.' With ruthless hands he stripped off her nightdress and tossed it aside.

A moment later she was quivering helplessly as, starting at her feet, his mouth began to move up her slim legs, planting soft baby kisses, lingering on the smooth skin on the insides of her knees and inner thighs as it moved inexorably towards its goal.

His lovemaking was prolonged and inventive and he wrung sensation after sensation from her, so piercingly sweet, so exquisite, that she was limp and shattered before he finally allowed her to sleep.

When she awoke in the morning, though it was quite early, she was alone in the big bed, the space beside her cold and empty.

Sitting up against the pillows, she sighed.

In spite of last night's attempt to put things right, the doubts and uncertainties Helen O'Connell's words had caused had driven a wedge between Richard and herself.

Though his lovemaking had been both skilful and passionate, she recognised unhappily that it had been fuelled by anger rather than love.

She sighed once more.

Today she was getting married. It should have been the most wonderful day of her life. *Would* have been the most wonderful day of her life if... But what earthly use was there in going over it all again?

She made an effort to focus on happier things.

In just a few hours she would be Richard's wife and tomorrow they would be going on their honeymoon. It seemed incredible. Everything had happened so quickly that not another soul knew.

Apart from Helen O'Connell...

She could hear the other woman's bitter laugh on being told, and her comment, 'I have to hand it to him. He said there was no time to lose, but I didn't think he could bring it off so soon.'

As the words echoed and re-echoed in her mind, Tina had a sudden vivid recollection of standing outside the living-room door yesterday morning, listening to the exchange between Richard and Helen.

Agitation making her heart beat faster, she went over in her mind everything she had overheard.

At the time she hadn't known what the argument was about. Now she did. Or at least to some extent.

Though she couldn't make heads nor tails of a lot of what had been said, it was clear that Helen had being trying to dissuade Richard from rushing into this marriage.

The quarrel had ended with her asking desperately, 'But have you considered the ethics of it?'

Richard had answered, 'You mean two wrongs don't make a right? Oh, yes, I've considered all that. But I'll do whatever it takes. As far as I'm concerned, the end justifies the means. I've far too much to lose to think of playing Sir Galahad...'

As Tina recalled the icy ruthlessness in his voice, shivers ran down her spine.

'I've far too much to lose...'

Though she still had no idea what it was he wanted from her, one thing was suddenly clear in her mind, until she knew the truth she couldn't marry him.

But obviously it was no use asking him; he wouldn't tell her. *Though Helen O'Connell might.* If she could find a way of getting to talk to the other woman without Richard knowing.

After some thought, Tina dismissed the idea of trying to phone. This was something that needed to be tackled face to face. But it must be three or four miles to Farrington Hall where the O'Connells lived and there wasn't much time…

How long would it take her to walk?

Too long.

Then it came to her in a flash. If she could sneak out of the house and get to the stables—rather than chance running into any of the servants, she would have to leave by the main entrance—she could say she wanted to ride and borrow Juno.

Scrambling out of bed, she picked up her discarded night-dress and hurried through to the guest room.

When she had showered and dressed in the trousers and silky shirt she had worn the previous morning, she went quietly down the stairs. She had just reached the hall when she heard the sound of a door opening and closing somewhere near at hand.

She froze, her heart beating fast.

After a moment or two when there was no sound of approaching footsteps, feeling like a criminal, she crept across the hall and out of the house.

Already the morning was warm and sunny and by the time she had hurried to the stables she was hot and out of breath.

Josh was in the yard moving some bales of hay while the two horses looked out of their stalls.

'Morning, miss.' He touched his forelock.

'Morning, Josh.'

'You'll be wanting a ride?'

'If it's no trouble?'

'Why, bless my soul, none at all. Juno's raring to go. I'll 'ave 'er saddled up in a trice.'

Passing Tina the riding hat she'd worn the previous day, he queried, 'Is Mr Richard following on?'

'No, he's… he's busy just at the moment.'

While the groom was saddling the mare, Tina pulled on the hat and, in an absolute fever of impatience, hovered by the mounting block. What would she do if Richard suddenly appeared?

But, to her great relief, he didn't and, a minute or so later, with a word of thanks to Josh, she was in the saddle and heading for Farrington Hall.

CHAPTER TEN

KNOWING roughly where the Hall lay but unsure of the exact route, Tina set off across the park until she reached a pleasant track that appeared to lead in the right general direction.

The going was smooth and easy and, after a hundred yards or so, she urged the mare to a canter for a while before dropping to a trot.

They had almost reached the perimeter of the park when she caught sight of a house in the distance surrounded by a stone wall and fronted by sloping green lawns. An oblong built of mellow stone with symmetrical rows of windows and chimneys and a porticoed entrance, it was solid-looking and stately rather than beautiful.

This had to be Farrington Hall.

Skirting a cattle grid, she opened a weighted gate to the right without dismounting and left the park to follow a quiet lane.

After a while she came to a grand gateway, but the gatehouse appeared to be unoccupied and the black wrought iron gates, flanked by stone pillars surmounted by huge stone balls, stood wide.

Subduing her qualms, she rode in and followed a carefully tended drive up to a paved apron and the front entrance. There she dismounted and, still holding the reins, rang a large old-fashioned bell. When the door was answered by a neatly dressed elderly housekeeper, Tina gave her name and asked to speak to Miss O'Connell.

'If you'll be good enough to wait there a moment, Miss Dunbar, I'll tell Miss Helen you're here and get young Tom to take care of your horse.'

She had been gone a minute or so when a young man in shirt sleeves appeared round the side of the house. As he said a civil, 'Good morning,' to Tina and took Juno's reins, Helen O'Connell appeared in the hall.

Looking as if Tina's unexpected visit had flustered her, she said shortly, 'I was just finishing breakfast. You'd better come through.'

Having led the way into a sunny morning room, she waved Tina to a chair and asked, 'Would you like some coffee?'

'No, thanks. I don't want to take up a lot of your time, but I need to know what you meant by, "…don't let yourself be conned; as soon as he's got what he wants…he'll divorce you".'

Helen's lips tightened. 'Try asking Richard.'

'Do you think he'd tell me?'

'I very much doubt it,' Helen admitted.

'You said, "…if all this trouble hadn't blown up he would have married me…" If you really believe that, and you don't want me to marry him, you'd better tell me what you meant by "all this trouble" and what it is he wants from me.'

'And if I don't?'

'Then I'll go ahead with the wedding. If you're so confident he'll divorce me, perhaps you—'

Her face contorted as though in pain, Helen cried, 'I don't believe in divorce.'

Tina felt sorry for the other woman but, reminding herself firmly that she *needed* to know, she said, 'Then it might pay you to tell me.'

'If I do, Richard will never forgive me.'

'He will if he cares at all for you.'

The other woman stayed silent and, realising she was beaten, Tina rose and was turning away when Helen said, 'Very well, I'll chance it. If he marries you, I've lost him anyway…

'It started when Bradley Sanderson died. He'd made a will leaving the castle to his daughter…'

'But I understood he hadn't got any children… And surely the castle wasn't his to—'

'That's just it—it *was*. He'd double-crossed Richard and left Anders to an illegitimate daughter no one knew he had.

'Apparently he'd had no contact with her and he didn't know where she was currently living. All he knew about her was her name, roughly how old she was and where she'd lived after being adopted, so it was left to his solicitors to trace her. Which they did, surprisingly quickly—'

'But I don't see what this has to—'

'*You're* Bradley Sanderson's daughter.'

As Tina gaped at her, deprived of speech, Helen went on, 'Richard realised that, once the solicitors had been in touch with you, it would be too late.

'He dreaded the thought of losing Anders and he decided that his best chance of keeping it under his control was to marry you before you learnt about your inheritance. That was the reason for all the haste.'

It made a terrible kind of sense, apart from one thing. Finding her voice, Tina said flatly, 'There's no way I can be Bradley Sanderson's daughter.'

For a moment Helen looked shaken. Then she said, 'The solicitors believe you are. They've already written to you…'

As Tina began to shake her head, Helen added, 'Richard told me he'd intercepted their letter.'

Recalling the unopened letter that had so mysteriously vanished, Tina felt shock hit her like a blow over the heart.

But she couldn't be Bradley Sanderson's daughter.

Though clearly Richard believed she was, and that was why

he'd tried to rush her into this marriage. Why he had wanted her to sign the paper saying that, if they were divorced, she relinquished any claim to the castle.

All the talk of love at first sight had only been a lie, a sham. He cared nothing for her. His only concern had been to safeguard his inheritance.

She was filled with pain, an agony so intense that it gripped her like an iron maiden, paralysing her heart and her lungs and making cold perspiration break out on her forehead.

After a moment or two the worst of the pain passed, leaving her cold and numb and empty, as though some vital life force had been extinguished.

Through stiff lips, she said, 'Thank you for telling me,' and made her way blindly across the hall and out to where Tom was waiting with Juno.

Having thanked him, she mounted and, thoughts tumbling through her mind, chaotic as clowns, set off back to the castle.

When she had returned Juno and the borrowed riding hat and assured Josh she'd had an enjoyable ride, she crossed the wooden bridge and went in through the rear entrance.

As she was crossing the servants' hall, Hannah appeared and, a look of relief on her face, said, 'Good morning, Miss Dunbar.'

'Good morning, Hannah.' Tina was pleased to find that her voice sounded relatively normal.

'Mr Richard will be glad to see you,' Hannah went on. 'He couldn't imagine where you'd got to.'

'Where is he now?'

'He's out looking for you. I'll send Mullins to tell him you're back...'

The grandfather clock in the corner wheezed asthmatically and struck nine-thirty.

'If you've changed your mind about needing any help with your wedding dress—' the housekeeper began.

'Thank you, Hannah, but I haven't. Perhaps you'll be kind

enough to ask Mullins to tell Mr Richard that I'll wait for him in his study?'

Leaving the housekeeper looking perplexed and uneasy, Tina squared her shoulders in preparation for the forthcoming confrontation and made her way to the study.

She had been there only a short time when the latch clicked and Richard came striding in.

He was smartly dressed in a grey suit and a matching silk shirt and tie, but for once his calm self-control was absent. He looked rattled, his face pale, his dark hair untidy, as though he'd been raking agitated fingers through it.

'Where the devil have you been?' he demanded urgently. 'I've looked everywhere for you.'

Steadily, she said, 'I took Juno and rode over to see Helen O'Connell. There were some questions I needed answers to.'

A shutter came down. 'And?'

'I got them.'

With a glance at his watch, he suggested, 'Perhaps we can discuss what Helen told you later? The Reverend Peter will be waiting.'

'Now I know *why* you want to marry me I've no intention of going through with the wedding,' she informed him quietly and held her breath, waiting for the storm.

It never came.

Just as quietly, he said, 'Then, if you'll excuse me for a few minutes, I'll let the Reverend Peter know that the ceremony is postponed.'

'*Cancelled.*'

His mouth twisted. 'It seems that Helen's done a good job.'

'As it's the truth, it isn't fair to blame *her*.'

'Are you quite satisfied that what she told you *is* the truth?'

Tina swallowed hard. 'Yes.'

He turned on his heel and left without a word.

Suddenly feeling limp and slightly sick, she sank down in the nearest chair.

She was still sitting staring unseeingly into space when he came back a few minutes later.

Glancing up at his entrance, she saw that he had regained his self-control and was now the cool, assured man she was used to.

Dropping into a chair opposite, he suggested levelly, 'Perhaps you'd better tell me exactly what Helen said.'

'At first she didn't want to say anything, but when I pushed her she told me that Bradley Sanderson had double-crossed you and left the castle to his illegitimate daughter.

'She said you thought that *I* was that daughter and you were trying to rush me into marriage before I discovered that I'd inherited the castle.'

His tawny eyes on her face, he asked, 'And do you believe that?'

'It's the truth, isn't it?'

'Yes,' he admitted.

'What did you intend to do when I discovered *why* you'd married me? Presumably you couldn't have hidden the reason for too long.'

'At first I wasn't sure,' he admitted. 'I told myself I would deal with that when it happened.

'Then, when I started to get to know you, I decided that as soon as we got back from our honeymoon I'd tell you everything. I hoped very much that when you knew the truth you'd stay with me.'

'Helen O'Connell was sure that you intended to divorce me and, as you'd got me to sign a paper giving up all rights to the castle—'

'That wasn't because I intended to divorce you,' he broke in. 'It was a precaution in case you wanted to divorce me.'

'If I had, you'd got everything sewn up quite nicely,' she said with some bitterness. 'And if I'd tried to take it to court, you had the necessary money and clout to make sure you'd win.'

Quietly, he said, 'Believe me, I'm not proud of the way I've acted. Everything I've done was done out of sheer desperation.'

All the pain she felt evident in her voice, she cried, 'I just don't see why you felt you had to marry me. There must have been some other way. It isn't as if you haven't got money—'

'Oh, yes, I've got money. But I couldn't be sure you'd be willing to sell the castle. And even if you *had* been willing, not knowing what kind of woman you were, I didn't want to find myself over a barrel and bled dry.'

'I would never have done such a thing.'

Leaning forward, he took her hand. 'Now I know you better, I'm sure you wouldn't. But there was no time to find out what kind of woman I was dealing with.

'I had to take drastic action in order to keep Anders. Apart from the fact that I love the old place, it's my heritage, my birthright.

'Please try to understand…'

'I do, in a way.'

Unsettled by his touch, she pulled her hand free before going on, 'What I *don't* understand is how Bradley was able to will it away from you.'

Richard sighed. 'As I told you, I'd agreed to my mother putting a codicil in her will giving him the right to live at the castle until his death.

'At the time he seemed satisfied with that, but when she became really ill he began to put pressure on her to change it. He told her it was his dearest wish to actually be master of the castle for the short time he had left. He added that he thought she owed it to him.

'Finally, when she couldn't hold out against him any longer, she agreed to do as he asked on condition that he then bequeathed it to me.

'Both those wills were formally drawn up by Alexander Fry, the family's solicitor.

'A few weeks later, Fry rang up and spoke to my mother. He asked if she knew that Bradley had been in and made another will.

'When she admitted that she hadn't known, he said, "I rather thought not".

'He added that he was unable to disclose the contents of the second will, but he thought she should be aware that it invalidated the first.

'Though she knew of no one Bradley would want to leave anything to, she was seriously concerned.

'She talked the whole thing over with Hannah and the Reverend Peter—that's how I came to learn about it—and, afraid that Bradley was planning something underhand, she decided to make a second will herself.

'By now she was far too ill to go out and she didn't want to arouse Bradley's suspicions by having Fry come to the house, so on a single sheet of parchment she wrote that she bequeathed everything she owned to me and got the Reverend Peter and Hannah to witness it—'

Tina gave a sigh of relief. 'Then I don't see what the problem is.'

'The problem is that second will can't be found. I would have expected her to have put it in her secret drawer, but it wasn't there. And, after an intensive search, it still hasn't come to light, so I can only presume that Bradley found it and destroyed it.'

'Oh,' Tina said in a small voice.

'But, as Mother intended me to have Anders and the castle has been in my family so long, I'm regarding it as mine until Bradley's will has been proven and probate granted. Then, unless I fight it through the courts, which may take years, it will be yours.'

She shook her head. 'That's just it—it won't.'

His head came up. 'What do you mean— it won't?'

'I'm not Bradley Sanderson's daughter. I couldn't possibly be. My parents had been married over a year when I was born.'

Wearily, he began, 'That doesn't—'

'I know what you're going to say. The fact that they'd been married over a year doesn't rule out the possibility that my mother had an affair with Bradley.

'But I don't believe she did. Apart from the fact that she'd been brought up to have good moral principles, she and my father adored each other. She would never have looked at another man.'

'What was she like? Do you take after her?'

Tina shook her head. 'She was small and dark, like the rest of her family, with a gentle face and big grey eyes.

'What about Bradley—what did he look like?'

'He was short and thickset. His hair was iron-grey when I knew him, but it had been dark and his eyes were brown.'

'My father is tall and fair and blue-eyed. Everyone used to say I was the spitting image of him. I have a photograph of us together and the likeness is unmistakable.

'So you see there's been some mix-up.'

Richard frowned. 'Dunbar isn't a particularly common name and the solicitors must have been satisfied they'd found the right woman.'

'Helen mentioned that they'd written to me and that you'd…intercepted the letter.'

'Yes.' He looked momentarily discomposed. 'I'm sorry, but I thought it necessary.'

'How did you manage it?' she asked curiously.

'I was at Cartel Wines, and I saw you leave your office at lunch time—'

All at once everything clicked into place like a blurred photograph coming into focus. 'So you were watching me…'

He didn't deny it.

'Go on,' she said tightly.

'I went in and noticed a letter lying on your desk with the solicitors' names stamped on it. I was thrown by the fact that they'd managed to trace you so quickly.

'When I looked at the letter and found you hadn't yet read it, I thanked my lucky stars.

'I was still wondering what to do for the best when, from your office window, I saw you coming back through the gates.

'I pocketed the letter and came down. I was considering taking the chance to speak to you.'

'So why didn't you?'

'A kind of gut instinct that the timing wasn't right. I decided to wait until after De Vere had given you the news.'

'So it was your doing. I suppose taking steps to see I had no job was a way of softening me up, making me vulnerable...'

'Partly,' he admitted honestly. 'Also I'd regarded it as one less avenue through which the solicitors could contact you.'

'I see... What I don't understand is why, that evening, you tried to scare me.'

He turned and looked at her, holding her gaze. 'I wasn't trying to scare you.'

'Then why were you in the warehouse watching me...?'

He shook his head. 'You were so long coming down I began to think I'd missed you. When the security man had finished his rounds I went back to check that you were still in your office and found you were just leaving.'

She looked down at her hands, unable to look up at him. 'So you followed me out to my car and ran into me on purpose. Why?'

He sighed, lifting her chin so their eyes met. 'Though I had several strategies in place, I'd banked on having considerably more time. And, even though I'd taken the letter, I knew it would only be a matter of days before you learnt the truth.

'I decided I had to take some action, and quickly. My hope was to drive you home and try to get to know you. It was a sheer stroke of luck that you had nowhere to sleep. The rest followed on from there...'

At the thought of what 'the rest' had been, she was filled with such anguish that for a moment she was unable to speak or move.

The whole thing had been just a sham. Lies and deception. And all for nothing.

Gritting her teeth against the onslaught of pain, she asked, 'Do you still have the solicitors' letter? It might provide an answer as to how the identity mix-up occurred.'

'I doubt it.' He got to his feet and, opening a drawer in his desk, took out a letter and handed it to her. 'Solicitors are usually too cautious to give much away.'

The envelope was addressed to Miss V Dunbar and in a red rectangle, opposite the franking, were the names Barnard, Rudge and Fry.

It was still sealed.

Her fingers just a shade unsteady, Tina tore it open and froze. After a stunned few seconds she read the cautiously phrased request that the recipient should contact them as soon as was convenient. The letter added that, after the necessary proof of identity had been provided, she would learn 'something to her advantage'.

'Well?' Richard asked. 'Does it provide an answer?'

'All the answer I need.' She handed him the letter.

He glanced through it, then said, 'They appear to have your given name wrong—'

'That's it exactly,' she broke in. 'It's headed Miss *Valerie* Dunbar…'

'It could be a secretarial mistake—'

'But it *isn't* a mistake. Had the envelope been addressed to Miss Valerie Dunbar, I would have known straight away that it wasn't for me.'

Richard was staring at her, his dark brows knitted.

'Don't you see; it's my stepsister who's Bradley's daughter! My stepmother once told me that she already had Valerie when she married her first husband.'

'You told me your stepsister was called Didi.'

'The family have always called her Didi, while her friends

all know her as Val. She hated the name Valerie and wouldn't let anyone use it.'

Richard's thoughts raced. It seemed the solicitors had found the right woman and it was his own detective who had got mixed up.

So was the dossier Grimshaw had drawn up a picture of Valerie or Valentina?

Almost certainly, Valerie. He felt an overwhelming gladness. He'd been misjudging Valentina from start to finish. She wasn't the 'anything goes' young woman he'd presumed.

And that explained so much.

The first night he'd taken her to bed and been startled into thinking he was making love to an inexperienced woman, he'd been right.

Not really needing confirmation, but deciding to dot the 'i's and cross the 't's, he said, 'Tell me about your stepsister. What's she like?'

'She's beautiful. Slim, about my height, blonde and blue-eyed.'

'Naturally blonde?'

'No. When she doesn't change her colour, her hair's quite dark.'

'What is she like in character? You told me you and she were very different.'

'We are.'

'In what way?'

Tina sighed. 'I was always the quiet introvert, whereas Didi was headstrong and reckless. While she was still at school she got in with the wrong crowd. Her mother was worried to death about her—'

'Drink and drugs and sex,' Richard said.

'How did you know?' Tina demanded.

'My detective checked back.'

Realisation dawning, she cried, 'And you thought it was me!'

'Yes,' he admitted steadily, 'I did at first. Though I soon

realised that nothing seemed to fit. You just didn't correspond with the picture he'd painted of you.

'The woman he described was bed-hopping when she was barely sixteen and since then she appears to have had numerous men in her life. While the only man you've mentioned was your fiancé.'

Then, frowning thoughtfully, 'I gather from what you've told me that your stepsister was living with you while you were engaged?'

'Yes.'

Watching Tina's face, noting her change of colour, he hazarded, 'Presumably she had something to do with the break-up?'

'I came home early one night and found them in bed together,' she told him flatly.

'And that's why you gave him his ring back.' It was a statement, not a question. 'What about her?'

'She said she was sorry. It hadn't been planned; it had just happened.'

'So you forgave her.'

'I always thought of her as being amoral rather than immoral.'

'Has she a boyfriend at the moment?'

'No one special that I know of. Why, were you intending to try to seduce and marry her?'

His jaw tightened as Tina's arrow went whang into the gold, but all he said was, 'You told me she was at drama school. I wondered who was paying her fees and supporting her...'

Tina remained silent, but suddenly recalling her saying, 'I have financial commitments that make it necessary to find another job without too much delay', he had his answer.

Carefully, he asked, 'How committed is she to the bright lights and becoming an actress?'

'I doubt if she would want to keep the castle, if that's what you mean. She always hated living in the country.'

'So you think she'll sell?'

'I'm sure of it. She's got her faults—haven't we all?—but greed isn't one of them, so if you offer her a fair price I believe she'll take it…'

His sigh of relief was audible.

'No doubt she'd squander it… But at least you'll have your home safe.'

Suddenly desperate to get away, she jumped to her feet and said, 'Now, if you'll please give me back my mobile…?'

He opened the top drawer of his desk and handed her the phone.

'Thanks.'

She turned to the door.

'Where are you going?' he asked sharply.

'Back to London to visit some employment agencies.' With a bitter little laugh, she added, 'I suggest you fire your so-called detective. If it hadn't been for him you wouldn't have wasted so much time and effort and I wouldn't be looking for another job…'

Richard caught her arm and brought her to a halt. 'Valentina, I—'

A knock cut through his words and he asked tersely, 'Who is it?'

Hannah came in, looking anxious and unhappy. 'I'm sorry to bother you, Mr Richard, but Cook would like to know what to do about meals…'

'You'd better tell her to serve lunch as usual.'

'And Miss O'Connell is asking to see you… She seemed very upset, almost hysterical.'

After a momentary hesitation he said, 'Very well. Perhaps you'll show her into the living-room?'

As Hannah turned to go, Tina pulled her arm free and made to follow her out.

'Wait,' Richard said. 'I need to talk to you.'

'As far as I'm concerned, there's nothing more to talk about. I intend to ring for a taxi and leave as soon as I've packed.'

'Valentina, listen to me,' Richard said urgently.

But, blinded by tears, she fled across the hall and up the stairs.

When she reached her room, she dashed the tears away with the back of her hand and, switching on her mobile, brought up the number of the Home Counties taxi firm.

Assured that a cab would be there within fifteen minutes, blinded by fresh tears, she began to push things higgledy-piggledy into her small case, trying to ignore the wedding dress that glimmered, pale and ghost-like, in the depths of the wardrobe.

Her packing finished, she was fastening the case when the ring she was still wearing caught the sun and flashed fire. Pulling it off, she hesitated for a moment, wondering where to leave the lovely thing. But somehow it seemed only right and proper to return it to its box.

She crossed to the writing desk and, as Richard had done, reached into the recess. After a moment, at either end her searching fingertips found a small, slightly raised area no larger than the head of a drawing pin. She pressed them simultaneously and the secret drawer slid open.

Taking out the velvet-covered box, which had previously held the three rings but was now empty, she put the solitaire back and returned the box to the drawer. But when she attempted to close it, the drawer slid part of the way and then stopped.

Realising that she couldn't have applied an even pressure, she tried once more.

But again it failed to close properly.

Wishing, now it was too late, that she had simply left the ring on the bedside cabinet, she tried for a third time to close the drawer.

Without success.

Wondering what was stopping it, she bent her head and peered inside. A small pale triangle right at the back of the drawer caught her eye. Something seemed to be trapped. But there was no way she could reach it, unless the drawer came right out.

After a moment's careful manoeuvring, she found it did, sliding free into her hands. Placing it carefully on the desk, she peered once more into the dimness of the recess.

Wedged in the small space behind the drawer was some crumpled paper that must have been caught and carried over the back. It might have stayed hidden there indefinitely if it hadn't somehow moved, preventing the drawer from closing properly.

Reaching in, she fished it out.

Though it was badly creased, the date and the writing were perfectly legible, as were the signatures of the two people who had witnessed it.

All she could feel was vast relief that justice would now be done.

She put her bag over her shoulder and her coat over her arm, then, her case in one hand and the will in the other, hurried out. She had just reached the head of the stairs when Richard and Helen came out of the living-room.

Standing like a statue, she watched him escort the other woman across the hall. He had an arm around her and they appeared to be the best of friends once more. Opening the door, he stooped and kissed her cheek. She gave him a fleeting smile as he followed her out.

After a second or two, Tina heard the sound of a car engine.

She had just reached the second stair from the bottom when Richard reappeared and crossed the hall to stand in her way.

'I suppose you saw Helen just leaving?'

'Yes,' she said.

'We had a talk and I told her how things stood, how I felt about you.'

'You appear to be good friends again.'

'Friends... Nothing more. She wished me well and said she hoped you'd stay.'

Looking him in the eye, Tina told him, 'The minute my taxi

gets here I'm going and you can't stop me. But first I wanted to give you this.'

She held out the crumpled piece of paper.

He took it from her and stared down at it for a moment, then he looked up, his handsome face suddenly alight. 'Thank you,' he said simply. 'Where did you find it?'

'It was wedged behind your mother's secret drawer. I was putting her ring back when I found it wouldn't close properly. When I looked to see why not, I found the will wedged in the gap behind the drawer and the back of the desk... So now you've got what you want...' She made to brush past him.

'Oh, but I haven't.' He thrust the will into his pocket and, taking the case from her hand, tossed it aside. A moment later her coat and bag joined it.

Then, sweeping her up in his arms, he carried her into the living-room and, dropping her unceremoniously on to the couch, sat down beside her, trapping her there.

'Let me go,' she said raggedly. 'My taxi will be waiting.'

He shook his head. 'It came when I was seeing Helen off and I sent it away.'

'How dare you send it away when I—?'

'Before you think of leaving, we need to talk.'

'I've already told you that, as far as I'm concerned, there's nothing more to talk about. I insist that you let me go this minute—'

He swooped and covered her mouth with his, stifling the angry words.

Only when she was limp and breathless did he raise his head. 'As far as you're concerned there may be nothing else to talk about, but you're going to stay and listen to what I have to say.

'First, however, I want to ask you something. Why did you bring the will to me?'

She looked at him blankly. 'I don't understand what you mean.'

'I mean that instead of giving it to me you could have destroyed it and made your stepsister rich.'

Horrified, she cried, 'What kind of woman do you think I am? Bradley had no right to the castle and Didi had no right to benefit from his perfidy. She would have been the first to admit that.

'As I told you before, she has her faults but she's neither dishonest nor mercenary. And, as she knows nothing about it, she won't grieve over it.'

'Even so, it will be my pleasure to make sure that her future is financially secure.

'Now, in answer to your question, I think you're honest and loyal and brave, the kind of woman that any man would be fiercely proud of and want to have in his life. I want you in mine.'

'If you imagine for one moment that—'

He put a finger to her lips. 'You have every right to be furious. I've treated you abominably. I've deceived you and lied to you. But not about everything. When I told you I'd fallen in love with you at first sight, it was true.

'My main fear was that when you discovered the truth you'd leave me. My only hope was that *you'd* said you loved *me*.

'Even when I thought the worst of you, I still wanted to marry you, wanted you to be my wife and the mother of my children.

'If I hadn't loved you and meant the marriage to be a permanent one I would never have suggested using my parents' rings...'

If she had needed any further proof that he meant what he said, that would have convinced her.

But when he went on with obvious sincerity, 'Anders means a great deal to me, but you mean more...' the last of her anger and resentment vanished and her heart swelled with love and gratitude.

He took her hand and held it tightly. 'If you don't marry me and live here with me for the rest of my life, I'll only be half alive.

'Say you can forgive me and let me start all over again. I'm willing to wait, to take things slowly this time.'

'I don't want to start all over again.'

She saw the naked despair in his face, the desolation he couldn't hide, and, putting the palm of her free hand against his cheek in the tenderest of gestures, went on. 'I love you. We have a priest and a chapel, a wedding dress and rings, so why wait? After all, we don't want to disappoint—'

The rest of the sentence was lost as he pulled her into his arms and began to kiss her.

When they finally drew apart a little, he said, a shade unsteadily, 'If the ceremony goes ahead as planned, then we won't disappoint Hannah.'

'I wasn't going to say Hannah,' she told him mischievously.

'Oh?' He raised a dark brow. 'Who *were* you going to say? The Reverend Peter?'

She shook her head. 'Our bed.'

Laughing, he pulled her back into his arms and said, 'My love, the way we feel about each other, we'll give it a whole new tale to tell.'

* * * * *

THE ROYAL HOUSE OF NIROLI
Always passionate, always proud

The richest royal family in the world—
united by blood and passion,
torn apart by deceit and desire

Nestled in the azure blue of the Mediterranean Sea, the majestic island of Niroli has prospered for centuries. The Fierezza men have worn the crown with passion and pride since ancient times. But now, as the king's health declines, and his two sons have been tragically killed, the crown is in jeopardy.

The clock is ticking—a new heir must be found before the king is forced to abdicate. By royal decree the internationally scattered members of the Fierezza family are summoned to claim their destiny. But any person who takes the throne must do so according to The Rules of the Royal House of Niroli. Soon secrets and rivalries emerge as the descendents of this ancient royal line vie for position and power. Only a true Fierezza can become ruler—a person dedicated to their country, their people…and their eternal love!

*Each month starting in July 2007,
Harlequin Presents is delighted to bring you
an exciting installment from*
THE ROYAL HOUSE OF NIROLI,
*in which you can follow the epic search
for the true Nirolian king.
Eight heirs, eight romances, eight fantastic stories!*

Here's your chance to enjoy a sneak preview of the first book delivered to you by royal decree…

FIVE minutes later she was standing immobile in front of the study's window, her original purpose of coming in forgotten, as she stared in shocked horror at the envelope she was holding. Waves of heat followed by icy chill surged through her body. She could hardly see the address now through her blurred vision, but the crest on its left-hand front corner stood out, its *royal* crest, followed by the address: *HRH Prince Marco of Niroli...*

She didn't hear Marco's key in the apartment door, she didn't even hear him calling out her name. Her shock was so great that nothing could penetrate it. It encased her in a kind of bubble, which only concentrated the torment of what she was suffering and branded it on her brain so that it could never be forgotten. It was only finally pierced by the sudden opening of the study door as Marco walked in.

"Welcome home, *Your Highness*. I suppose I ought to curtsy." She waited, praying that he would laugh and tell her that she had got it all wrong, that the envelope she was holding, addressing him as Prince Marco of Niroli, was some silly mistake. But like a tiny candle flame shivering vulnerably in the dark, her hope trembled fearfully. And then the look in Marco's eyes extinguished it as cruelly as a hand placed callously over a dying person's face to stem their last breath.

"Give that to me," he demanded, taking the envelope from her.

"It's too late, Marco," Emily told him brokenly. "I know the truth now…." She dug her teeth in her lower lip to try to force back her own pain.

"You had no right to go through my desk," Marco shot back at her furiously, full of loathing at being caught off-guard and forced into a position in which he was in the wrong, making him determined to find something he could accuse Emily of. "I trusted you…."

Emily could hardly believe what she was hearing. "No, you didn't trust me, Marco, and you didn't trust me because you knew that I couldn't trust you. And you knew that because you're a liar, and liars don't trust people because they know that they themselves cannot be trusted." She not only felt sick, she also felt as though she could hardly breathe. "You are Prince Marco of Niroli…. How could you not tell me who you are and still live with me as intimately as we have lived together?" she demanded brokenly.

"Stop being so ridiculously dramatic," Marco demanded fiercely. "You are making too much of the situation."

"Too much?" Emily almost screamed the words at him. "When were you going to tell me, Marco? Perhaps you just planned to walk away without telling me anything? After all, what do my feelings matter to you?"

"Of course they matter." Marco stopped her sharply. "And it was in part to protect them, and you, that I decided not to inform you when my grandfather first announced that he intended to step down from the throne and hand it on to me."

"To protect me?" Emily nearly choked on her fury. "Hand on the throne? No wonder you told me when you first took me to bed that all you wanted was sex. You *knew* that was the only kind of relationship there could ever be between us! You *knew* that one day you would be Niroli's king. No doubt you are expected to marry a princess. Is she picked out for you already, your *royal* bride?"

* * * * *

Look for THE FUTURE KING'S PREGNANT MISTRESS
by Penny Jordan in July 2007,
from Harlequin Presents,
available wherever books are sold.

THE ROYAL HOUSE OF NIROLI

Always passionate, always proud.

**The richest royal family in the world—
a family united by blood and passion,
torn apart by deceit and desire.**

Step into the glamorous, enticing world of the
Nirolian Royal Family. As the king ails he must find an
heir…each month an exciting new installment follows
the epic search for the true Nirolian king. Eight heirs,
eight romances, eight fantastic stories!

It's time for playboy prince Marco Fierezza to
claim his rightful place…on the throne of Niroli!
Emily loves Marco, but she has no idea he's a royal
prince! What will this king-in-waiting do when he
discovers his mistress is pregnant?

THE FUTURE KING'S PREGNANT MISTRESS

by Penny Jordan

(#2643)

On sale July 2007.

www.eHarlequin.com

HP12643

REQUEST YOUR FREE BOOKS!

◆ HARLEQUIN® *Presents* ®

2 FREE NOVELS
PLUS 2
FREE GIFTS!

PASSION GUARANTEED SEDUCTION

YES! Please send me 2 FREE Harlequin Presents® novels and my 2 FREE gifts. After receiving them, if I don't wish to receive any more books, I can return the shipping statement marked "cancel." If I don't cancel, I will receive 6 brand-new novels every month and be billed just $3.80 per book in the U.S., or $4.47 per book in Canada, plus 25¢ shipping and handling per book and applicable taxes, if any*. That's a savings of close to 15% off the cover price! I understand that accepting the 2 free books and gifts places me under no obligation to buy anything. I can always return a shipment and cancel at any time. Even if I never buy another book from Harlequin, the two free books and gifts are mine to keep forever.

106 HDN EEXK 306 HDN EEXV

Name _____ (PLEASE PRINT) _____

Address _____ Apt. # _____

City _____ State/Prov. _____ Zip/Postal Code _____

Signature (if under 18, a parent or guardian must sign)

Mail to the **Harlequin Reader Service®**:
IN U.S.A.: P.O. Box 1867, Buffalo, NY 14240-1867
IN CANADA: P.O. Box 609, Fort Erie, Ontario L2A 5X3

Not valid to current Harlequin Presents subscribers.

Want to try two free books from another line?
Call 1-800-873-8635 or visit www.morefreebooks.com.

* Terms and prices subject to change without notice. NY residents add applicable sales tax. Canadian residents will be charged applicable provincial taxes and GST. This offer is limited to one order per household. All orders subject to approval. Credit or debit balances in a customer's account(s) may be offset by any other outstanding balance owed by or to the customer. Please allow 4 to 6 weeks for delivery.

Your Privacy: Harlequin is committed to protecting your privacy. Our Privacy Policy is available online at www.eHarlequin.com or upon request from the Reader Service. From time to time we make our lists of customers available to reputable firms who may have a product or service of interest to you. If you would prefer we not share your name and address, please check here. ☐

HP07

Mediterranean NIGHTS™

Tycoon Elias Stamos is launching his newest luxury cruise ship from his home port in Greece. But someone from his past is eager to expose old secrets and to see the Stamos empire crumble.

Mediterranean Nights
launches in June 2007 with...

FROM RUSSIA, WITH LOVE
by *Ingrid Weaver*

Join the guests and crew of *Alexandra's Dream* as they are drawn into a world of glamour, romance and intrigue in this new 12-book series.